WESTERN VENGEANCE

WESTERN VENGEANCE

LAURAN PAINE

SAGEBRUSH
Large Print Westerns

First published in Great Britain by Foulsham
First published in the United States by ISIS Publishing Ltd

Published in Large Print 2005 by ISIS Publishing Ltd,
7 Centremead, Osney Mead, Oxford OX2 0ES
United Kingdom
by arrangement with
Golden West Literary Agency

British Library Cataloguing in Publication Data
Paine, Lauran
    Western vengeance. – Large print ed. –
    (Sagebrush western series)
    1. Western stories
    2. Large type books
    I. Title
    813.5'4 [F]

ISBN 0–7531–7296–8 (hb)

Printed and bound by Antony Rowe, Chippenham

CHAPTER
ONE

"You'll be safe here," the bearded man said, sallow cheeks looking paler under the black shininess of his eyes. "For a time anyway. I don't think they'll dare break in here."

The younger man's sweat streaked face was grey under the dirt smudges. His eyes were dry-burning. "You saved my life, mister," he said. "They're out to lynch me for sure."

The black eyes had something cruel, fanatical, in them when the bearded man answered. "Keep your thanks. I don't want thanks from the likes of you. You're a murderer, but I believe in the right of the law, not the rope. Now stay here. Don't move." He straightened up, thick shoulders erect, heavy legs planted wide, his lingering black gaze shiny and uncompromising. For a moment longer he looked at the weasel-faced youth in his ragged clothes, saw the nakedness of a soul in the terrified blue eyes, then turned and left the room.

Outside a roar like floodwater, low and menacing, penetratingly ominous, filled the little town. The bearded man with the black eyes hesitated behind his door listening. His eyes fell to the latch, wavered. He turned back, went into a room off the parlour, took up a .31 calibre Colt pistol, dropped it into his black coat pocket and went back to the door, grasped the latch and pulled.

Slanting sunlight burnished the tops of buildings, but the dusty roadway, the shop-fronts, were in mauve shadows. The town ran a thousand feet south of him, two thousand feet northward. Under the overhang above the hard-walk were men. They were out in the heat cowed road too. Some were yelling like Indians but most of them were coming directly towards him like a slow avalanche; putting one foot down, then putting the other foot in front of it.

It was no drunken lynch-mob, he could see that. Faces he knew were under wide-brimmed hats. Jenks Burton of Cinnebar Ranch, Bob Downey of Welton's Stage and Express Company, Will Saunders from Willow Creek country. His breath ran shallow, his heart beat sturdily. They had right, in a sense, but not legal right. He'd said a thousand times that no land was better than its citizens' belief in the law.

It wasn't the sight of the men, it was the sound and bulkiness of their approach. Not drunkenly disorderly, but solidly packed and steady-eyed.

"Hey, Judge — where'd he go?"

Will Saunders in from his Willow Creek horse ranch, called it out and the judge didn't answer.

From farther back in the mob a man yelled something uncomplimentary about Judge Anderson. Someone else growled for him to shut up. They closed their ranks a little, coming closer, concentrating on the bearded, black-eyed man with the bulging coat pocket,

2

the set jaw and unwavering stare. Jenks Burton stopped five feet away. He looked at the judge a moment before he spoke.

"He came down this way, Judge." Another pause, a sharpening of Jenks' hard blue eyes. "Did you see him?"

Before the judge could answer Will Saunders and Bob Downey pushed up. Will said, "He didn't break out o' town so he's got to be hidin' down here amongst the houses somewhere." Will was lanky, confident, harsh looking. He turned a cold stare on Judge Anderson. "Goin' to hang him, Judge. No court, no trial — just hang him."

Bob Downey, thick shouldered, shorter than the others and freshly shaven, Holbrook's manager for the Welton Company, looked disapprovingly up at Will Saunders and said something under his breath.

Jenks Burton hadn't moved. He was watching the judge steadily, thoughtfully. "Seen him, Judge?" He asked sharply.

Others thronged up, the noise died, some of the men hung back seeing the judge standing there, thick body towards them, coal black eyes glinting, chin-whiskers jutting, adamant.

Jenks Burton's mind closed down around two things. One, Judge Anderson's coat bulged. He had a gun and everyone knew he never used firearms, was against them. And, he hadn't spoken, hadn't answered. Jenks felt something, a suspicion. When Will Saunders started to move past, Jenks threw an arm out stopping him.

"Where is he, Judge?"

The black eyes fixed themselves on Jenks' face, studied the low, massive jaw, the tapering cheekbones, the almost slanted eyes and the tugged-low brim of Jenks' black hat.

"Aw," Will Saunders said, "let's go."

"Just a minute," Judge Anderson said sharply. "That man was being held in custody. He's to have a —"

"He ain't in custody no more," someone called out defiantly. "We took him out an' he broke away. Run down here somewhere. Won't be no trial now, Judge — no sir — Ol' Judge Lariat's goin' to stretch his neck. You better get back out —"

"Listen to me!" The black eyes flamed, the beard quivered. "This town's had its last lynching. You men go back where you came from."

Will Saunders made an ugly laugh. "An' let the whelp go? Not on your hidebound life we won't."

"There's law here," Judge Anderson yelled as they began to growl again. "That man will be tried according to the law. Now break this up — go on."

Jenks Burton threw up an arm. The noise subsided, a throaty undertone lingered, deep and rumbling. "Wait a minute, fellers," Jenks called out. "Just a minute." He dropped his arm. The suspicion in his eyes had crystallised, become something solid and bleak. In a lowered tone he said, "Judge — where is he?"

"Aw, don't waste time on this old cuss," Saunders said starting to move on. "He'll get plumb away. Come on Jenks, Bob, you other fellers. Spread out and comb the houses and yards down here. We'll get him. Afoot he can't get far."

4

"Just a damned minute," Jenks said again, voice rising, an edge coming into it. "Hold on a second. Judge here knows where the little whelp went — don't you Judge? Where?"

Anderson put a thick hand into his coat pocket. The fingers curled around the .31 calibre pistol, gripped it powerfully. "Whatever that man did he is the law's responsibility, not yours. Now beat it. Get out of here and stop this nonsense."

"Nonsense? Why, Judge — ."

"Shut up, Will," Jenks said.

Those far back were edging around the sides to see what was going on. The entire press of sweaty bodies moved in closer and Jenks moved solidly in the forefront. His stare never once shifted.

"Judge," there was earnestness and danger in Jenks' voice. "Judge, where'd you hide him?"

"Burton," Judge Anderson said, thumb crooking over the hammer of the pistol in his pocket, straining a little. "I'm warning you."

"No you aren't," Jenks said, stopping three feet away, head inched forward, jaw thrust out, heavy, obdurate looking. "You aren't warning me, Judge. It's the other way around. I'm warning you. If you get in our way there's going to be some feathers ruffled — your feathers, Judge."

"You fool," Anderson said. "What right did you have to take that prisoner out of the jailhouse? Don't you realise what you're doing; the bunch of you? You're interfering with the processes of the law. You're committing a crime."

"And what did *he* commit?" Jenks said. "Held up Bob's stage and shot the driver. You knew Hal Simpson as well as we did. Hal and Miz' Simpson and their three kids. This rotten little runt killed Harold Simpson, Judge. Processes of the law or not he's going to get hung for that and we're not waiting six months for you to decide whether to hang him or turn him loose." Jenks stopped speaking, his nostrils quivered, his small, slitted eyes, dirty-blue, piercing, flicked over the Judge's house. "Where'd you hide him, Judge? Don't lie because we'll — ."

Stung, Judge Anderson swore a sizzling oath, his eyes danced with contempt. "Lie! Lie to the likes of you! I've never lied to a lynch-mob yet and I won't start now. You bunch of — !"

"Nev' mind that kind of talk, Judge," Will Saunders said. He looked from Jenks Burton to Judge Anderson and back again. "Jenks; you think he's got him — hid him, maybe?"

"That's exactly what I think," Jenks said. "He either knows where the skunk is or he's got him hid himself. Go ahead, Judge — you never lied to a lynch-mob — tell me I'm lying."

Judge Anderson looked at Bob Downey. "What's got into you, Bob?" He said acidly. "Mingling with this scum. Go on back to your office before you're committed by the things they're doing."

Downey, pale, uncertain looking, the fierceness dying out of his eyes, his expression, stood irresolute and silent.

Judge Anderson tilted his head. "The rest of you — go on, now. Go on before it's too late. If you hang that outlaw you'll be equally guilty with him. Remember that. Go on — move along."

A few men moved off, shuffling away. A stalwart youth with a wild shock of brittle yellow hair, sun-bleached to silver, turkey-red face and an up-curving mouth, full and reckless, shouldered his way through the ranks and emerged into the clearing between Jenks Burton and Will Saunders. He was another Cinnebar outfit rider; his name was Nevada Wheaton. With devilment in his eyes and a challenging grin he said, "You reckon the old devil's got him hid in his house, Jenks?"

Burton didn't answer for a moment. "I think he knows something, Nevada," he said finally, watching the Judge.

"Well, then," Wheaton said, still smiling, "let's find out. Start with his damned house."

The .31 Colt cleared Judge Anderson's pocket and made a brittle, cocking sound. Wheaton's smile dissolved. He turned just his head and looked. Jenks Burton's shoulders drooped a little. Will Saunders, in the act of turning towards the crowd, stopped in mid-motion. Bob Downey's hung head snapped up, eyes big and getting bigger.

Jenks said, "Don't make — ."

"Shut up! All of you shut up and listen to me. This has gone far enough. Too far. Now, for the last time I'm going to tell you to disperse. If you don't I'll file a

7

complaint against every man here whose face I recognise."

"Put up that gun, Judge," Will Saunders said, coming full around, his face tight.

The judge ignored him. "Go on now; this is your last chance."

"Judge — goddamn you — *put up that gun!*"

The words crackled, drew Judge Anderson's attention back to Will Saunders. "You too, Saunders," he said harshly. "Your reputation's bad enough, don't make it any worse."

"Wait a second," Bob Downey said, moving in a little closer, all the colour gone out of his face. "Will, wait."

"Bob, get out of the way and shut up. Judge — you ain't got a chance," Saunders said. Some of the mob was moving away, thinning out. The argument had cooled them. They knew Judge Anderson. Twenty-odd years presiding over Holbrooks's legal entanglements, a fair, hard man, as honest as new money, uncompromising. What was happening before their eyes looked out of place, off-key. Old Judge Anderson with a gun in his fist facing twenty or so lynchers. More straggled off, a few grumbling, believing they should hang Hal Simpson's murderer but not believing it strongly enough to shoot the judge or get shot by him over it.

Will Saunders, Jenks Burton, Nevada Wheaton, and Bob Downey were still facing the black-eyed, bearded man, and his little .31 pistol.

"He came to you, didn't he?" Jenks said. "Lousy killer ran to the law, didn't he?"

"The law," Judge Anderson said, gripping the gun until his knuckles turned white, "is to protect people until they're adjudged."

"A murderer?" Wheaton said scornfully, his mouth drawn down.

"I don't believe in that kind of law, Judge."

"You'd better learn to, cowboy," Anderson said fiercely, "because it's the same law that protects *you*."

"No law that protects murderers is good enough for me, Judge."

Jenks Burton still stared at the older man, still held himself in his slight crouch. "Where is he, Judge; in the house?"

Nevada Wheaton cursed. "Let's go see."

The little pistol swung to bear on the big rider's belt buckle. "Without a warrant to search my house," the judge said firmly, "none of you'll get past the door."

"You're crazy, Judge," Will Saunders said softly. "Nuttier'n a pet 'coon. Now I'm telling you for the last time — *put up that gun!*"

"You don't tell me *anything*, Saunders!"

"Wait a second," Bob Downey said in a high, brittle voice. "Will — Jenks — wait a second."

"What for?" Jenks said.

"Give him a chance."

"We are," Jenks said evenly. "Giving him every chance in the world. Will's told him to put up his gun. We aren't crowdin' him."

"Yeah, but — ."

9

"Ain't no buts," Saunders said. "Judge — you got ten seconds to shed that gun and get away from that front door."

"You heard what I said, Saunders. You or no one like you'll ever order me to do anything. Not by a damned sight. Jenks — you'd better take your Cinnebar riders and Saunders and go along with the rest of your lynch-mob."

"He's in the house, isn't he?" Jenks said, straightening up. "Nevada, come here."

The big cowboy looked at Judge Anderson's gun then turned his back on it, went over where Jenks whispered something to him. Nevada went past the others walking south, muscling his way through the little throng that remained, not as lynch-conscious as it had been, rooted to the sun-baked roadway by drama.

Judge Anderson watched Nevada walk away. He licked his lips, assailed by uneasiness. An almost imperceptible movement on the part of Will Saunders brought his attention back. Jenks Burton spoke quickly.

"Hold it, Will. Just hold it."

Saunders' long arms were hooked, his right fingers fanned out a little. He didn't move after Jenks spoke. Judge Anderson's pistol was pointing directly at him and Bob Downey was turned to stone, mouth hanging open. One of the bystanders said, "Will's chock full o' guts." Another voice strained, not so high and excited said: "Guts're no match for the drop, you fool."

Jenks Burton had the initiative. His eyes had a more pronounced slant when he concentrated. "Judge — you got no right to hide that prisoner."

"Who has a better right?" Anderson demanded, watching Will Saunders and knowing he couldn't miss at six feet.

"The Marshal," Jenks said. "He's the only one's got the right to confine a man — not you or me."

For a fraction of a second Judge Anderson's black eyes flashed at Jenks Burton. His words were dry. "You're stalling, Jenks. I know you too well."

Jenks laughed and before the sound died a roaring shout and a long, piercing scream erupted from behind the judge. Anderson's shoulders twitched but he didn't look away from Will Saunders.

Men scuffled and yelled, and in primitive response to the barbarism other men hollered back until the road was full of noise, like it had been before. Judge Anderson felt the reverberations underfoot, in the hard-walk planking, then the door of his house was yanked violently inwards. Nevada Wheaton and two other Cinnebar riders emerged. They had the escaped prisoner. His face was white, eyes bulging and a dark red bruise stood out.

Judge Anderson hesitated and Jenks Burton said, "Nevada — stay behind the old devil."

They jerked the murderer to a halt. He said something in a broken voice to the judge. Will Saunders' voice drowned it out.

"Anderson! You better put up that gun!"

The judge was swinging his head frontward when Bob Downey yelled, swung his shoulder and knocked Saunders off balance. "Jenks; stop him!"

"Damn you, Downey." Saunders staggered, lips pulled away from his teeth. "You — !"

"Saunders!" The little gun was tilted but the lanky man completed his pivot and a long, looping arm flailed out. Bob Downey threw up an awkward guard, too late. The blow landed high, slantingly, and Downey lost his balance, quick-stepped backwards. Judge Anderson was moving, short, thick legs propelling him towards the taller, younger man. Jenks Burton moved too late to intervene if that had been his intention.

It happened too fast to see.

The judge was raising his gun like a club near Will Saunders' head when the horse rancher, motivated by instinct, whirled and ducked low, right hand moving like quicksilver towards his holstered gun. Anderson's arm was still rising. Nevada Wheaton spun into another Cinnebar rider, knocked him flat and sprawling and kept on moving, getting clear. Saunders' gun went off with a rocking explosion. There was no echo to the solitary shot. It was muffled by Judge Anderson's body.

Bob Downey's head was coming up when Saunders fired. He saw it; saw Judge Anderson's coat burst into shreds with fingers of fire running up it. Saw the judge's thick body hurled backwards until it fell solidly where Nevada Wheaton had been standing.

A Cinnebar rider was rolling frantically in the dust to get clear and the prisoner was running as hard as he could down the middle of the roadway. Jenks Burton drew his own gun in no hurry, threw it up almost to eye-level, arm out and bent, tracking the fleeing man. When he fired the murderer bounded into the air and fell hard. A gust of dark-tawny dust blew up all around him. He screamed. Nevada Wheaton went towards him gun in hand.

Bob Downey looked at Judge Anderson. A steady-pumping, heavy freshet of blood was running out of his mouth. The black eyes looked straight up at the faded sky, never blinked, never wavered, until they dulled, dust settled on them and no moisture came from within to carry it away. Downey moved on legs like stumps, knelt and patted out the tongues of gunpowder-flame.

"Judge . . . ?"

Jenks Burton holstered his gun and looked out where Nevada Wheaton stood. "Nevada? Is he dead?"

"Naw. Leg's broke though, it looks like."

"What I aimed for," Jenks said, and started out into the road.

What was left of the mob moved wide around Judge Anderson's body. Will Saunders was in it. Most of the men hung back, looking at the body. A killing usually had a sobering effect; it did now.

Bob Downey stood up and stepped across the body, leaned against the warped front of Fundemeyer's Emporium and looked sick. An old rider, bent, warped and wizened, shuffled closer, peering downward. "Is he dead?" he asked. Downey didn't answer him.

"Over here," someone yelled out. They were dragging the bloody-legged killer of stagedriver Simpson towards the three big cottonwoods that stood, or rather leaned, in the barn-lot of the Widow Taney's place.

"Hang his head in a weepin' willow tree
Never, never more his kin to see . . ."

"Downey — I untied 'em."

Bob Downey didn't answer.

The man went closer, touched his arm. "I untied 'em. Marshal an' his deputy. Deputy's pretty banged up but the Marshal's coming down."

Downey nodded and raised his left hand to point. "Look," he said.

Ten or twelve men were steadying Simpson's killer on the back of a commandeered horse. His arms were bent back and bound, his legs hung free on either side of the horse. There were shouts and Jenks Burton was pulling Will Saunders aside, talking to him. The doomed man's face with its purpling bruise was as grey as slate, his eyes were pinched down hard, closed. He didn't sag. Downey knew he hadn't fainted.

"*Now!*"

Someone hit the horse. It leapt ahead flinging up dust and dirt. The fall wasn't more than four feet. The killer's feet didn't quite touch the ground and his neck didn't break. Men cursed and jumped clear of the threshing legs then silence as deep as night settled. No one moved. The dying man's face turned purple, his eyes bulged, his mouth worked and the spasms of strangulation convulsed him. Bob Downey turned away. The man standing beside him said "Chriz'!" in a husky, rattling voice, and stood spellbound.

Voices guttered like weak candlelight around Bob Downey as he walked away. Men stood well back under

14

the overhang watching the murderer die. There was awe and distress in the sounds they made. An elderly man stopped in front of Downey.

"Bob."

He looked up, saw the face, the odd-shaped little badge on his mussed blue shirt. "Marshal. It's all over."

"Is that Judge Anderson yonder on the walk?"

"Yes."

"Is he shot? What happened?"

Downey shook his head. "I don't know. He told them to go on home — a lot of things. They wouldn't. He had the killer hidden in his house. They found him, brought him out — someone shot the judge."

"Is he dead?"

"Yes."

The marshal shifted his gaze. The body hung limply in the air. Someone had pulled it higher after death. It turned once around and back again as the coiledness of the lariat worked itself out. "Shot the judge and hung the Kid," he said slowly with great finality.

"What kid?"

"The Verde River Kid. That's what he was called. His real name was Eustace Carmody." The marshal looked at the spiralling body again then dropped his gaze to the dark inertness of Judge Anderson. A hopelessness settled over him. He looked southward over the town. Men stood in little groups, in pairs, individually, saying little, gazing at the two corpses. The wildness of moments before was gone, burnt out, numbness remained.

15

"They hurt Houston pretty bad. Someone gave him a hell of a crack over the skull. I walked him over to Doc's place." The hopelessness was heavy in Marshal Harry Mather's voice. "I'm going to quit, Bob. I had enough."

Downey didn't reply.

"Judge Anderson . . ."

Downey started to walk past.

"Bob, send Doc back up here will you? I'll go cut the Kid down an' see what can be done for the judge."

Downey didn't reply. He was conscious of men standing back in shadows as he progressed down the hard-walk. The town was sunk in a deep, unnerving silence and he had no strength left to care.

Up in the middle of town where a mottled sycamore stood before the Saddle & Harness shop, Doctor Tobey Harding spoke to him in his dry, sardonic voice.

"Good day's work, Bob. Who's the other one lying up there on the walk?"

"Judge Anderson."

Harding's eyes lost their sheen of hardness, widened in shock. "No," he said swiftly. "Not Carl Anderson."

"Marshal wants to see you up there."

"Is he alive?"

"No — the judge isn't."

"Who shot him?"

Downey shook his head and went on past, turned in at the doorway of the Welton Stage & Express Company's office and let the coolness of the gloomy little room surfeit him. AnnaLee looked at him from across the ancient counter. Her heavy eyebrows were up a little, the smokey-blackness of her eyes darker, unblinking.

"He's lynched, isn't he?"

"Yes."

"Do you feel better now, Bob?"

"I . . ." He dropped down at his desk. "Something happened. It got out of hand some way."

"What do you mean?" She bent a long look at him. Being his sister she knew his moods, expressions. There was something in his face she hadn't ever seen there before. "Bob; what happened?" He didn't answer and she crossed to his desk, stood in front of it erectly, gazing down at him. A premonition stirred within her. "Bob?"

"Judge Anderson got killed."

Her breath snagged, hung up then came out in a short burst. "No," she said in a loud whisper. "Oh, no, Bob."

"It happened fast. I — I've got to think about it. Sort it out in my mind — just exactly what happened."

"But why the judge? How did he get mixed up in it?"

"He had the killer hidden in his house." He looked up at her. "I don't want to talk about it any more right now, Ann."

She stood over him like a full-bodied statue. The dying sun hurled a blood-red bolt over the town. Some of the reflection got snarled in her red-gold hair and shone there. The rounded fullness of her blouse with the little gold watch-locket pinned on it stood out starkly white in the room.

Holbrook lay hushed and brooding in the early evening. People passed by on the hard-walk, unspeaking. Horsemen clattered by, wagons moved sluggishly, early lamps were lit and orange patches of light ran in liquid colour out into the wide roadway. Life went on, people pursued their patterns of existence, but in a voiceless, noiseless way.

AnnaLee Downey closed the books, checked off the schedule sheets, the passenger tabs, express bills-of-ladings, prolonged the little routine things waiting for her brother to get out of his chair and when he didn't move she leaned on the counter in the gloom looking steadily out through the window at the shadowy road and the buildings across the way. When she spoke it was as though she were alone.

"It was so senseless. Why did you have to get mixed up in it? He would have been hanged anyway. Everyone liked Harold Simpson. And Judge Anderson . . . Men are so thoughtless. So cruel. Why should a man like Carl Anderson be killed over a murderer like that?" She drew in a big breath and let it out again. "He had enough unhappiness in his life. What a terrible thing to have happen to him. How unfair, Bob. Remember when his wife died; how long it took her, wasting away, dying every day for two years? Remember how Jason was, wild and never staying home?"

Downey arose and shook himself, put a hand on his desk, saw the papers there and turned away in distaste. "Let's go home," he said.

They went down through the fragrant night, southward to the house on Lincoln Street their parents

18

had left them. AnnaLee went into the kitchen while Bob mechanically lit the coal-oil lamps, wandered aimlessly through the house followed by his thoughts and the vivid picture of black eyes staring upwards in an unyielding, vanquished way, into the saffron sky of day's end.

He went out onto the back porch with the smell of night, the town, and early spring flowers around him. His father's old rocker was there. He felt for it, dropped down, fumbled for tobacco and papers, made a cigarette and lit it, exhaled a great gust of smoke and leaned back. Shock, he told himself. You can't remember what happened because of the shock. Faces; Jenks Burton, Will Saunders, Nevada Wheaton, the judge, Verde River Kid, faces galore, noise, dust, shadows from a dying day, dust, a feverish madness and more faces — all in the haze of dust. Patting out the fingerlings of gun-flame on the judge's rusty old black coat. Behind it all the putty-dead face of Hal Simpson when the stage had come in. Hal inside, glazed, limp, a passenger wheeling the vehicle.

"Here. Drink this coffee, Bob."

He made no move to take it from her, but her presence reminded him of the things she'd said at the office. He thought back down the years to Mrs. Anderson, the lingering, cruel way death had toyed with her, then took her. And Jason Anderson. He'd grown up in Holbrook like the rest of them, but Jase had been different. When he and Will Saunders and AnnaLee, half a dozen others, had been exploring the world of youth Jase had been following the wagons, the

19

roundups, breaking horses, running with the horse-hunters, the riders, the big outfits. Jase had come to manhood early. Experience had made him worlds apart from others his age. He wore a gun at seventeen, trailed over to Tombstone at eighteen, was gone from home at nineteen, had never returned to Holbrook and when Mrs. Anderson died the judge stood alone except for old friends at the graveside.

"Bob; drink this."

He stubbed out the cigarette, took the coffee and saw his sister's silhouette in the gloom, the white blouse, the full dark skirt, the pale expressionless of her strong, handsome face, moving in a blur towards another chair on the porch.

It was scalding hot. His face pinched down against the sharp pain of the first swallow. He set the cup aside.

"Which one of them shot him?"

"I don't know," he said.

"You saw it, didn't you? You *must* know, Bob."

"Well; I can't remember, that's all. It happened so suddenly."

"Who else was there?"

He put his head far back on the high rest of the old chair and rocked slightly. "Seemed like half the town was there. I'm not sure who I recognised but — ."

"You left the office with Jenks Burton. He was a ring-leader. Did he kill Judge Anderson?"

"I don't know, Ann. I can't remember who shot, exactly. Seems like it wasn't Jenks, though."

"You've got to remember, Bob. It was bad enough to break into the jail and take that man out and lynch him, but killing Judge Anderson isn't going to be forgotten. When the mob went past after the murderer escaped from it I saw Ferris Whitley and Jake Untermeyer running south. Will Saunders was with them."

"No," he said. "No, it wasn't Ferris or Jake. When the judge started talking Jake turned back. Ferris came up later and told me he'd untied the marshal and Houston Mabry. He wasn't there when Anderson got shot, I remember that. He stood beside me in front of Fundemeyer's when they strunk the Kid up."

Her eyes, the colour of smoke from a tipi on a wintery day, swung. "Bob; was it you?"

He rolled his head on the back of the chair. "Not me, Ann. I didn't have a gun."

"You've *got* to remember. The government will send U.S. Marshals here, Bob. People know you were in the mob — right up in the front of it. They might even say you shot him."

"That's silly," he said, but the idea grew and flourished in his mind and his answer sounded a little hollow, lacking conviction. "You know I don't wear a gun in town. Everybody knows it."

"That won't stop people from saying you had one today."

"Ann, stop talking about it will you?"

She turned her head, gazed out into the darkness with a troubled expression. "It was so senseless, Bob. So utterly senseless. If you men had taken up a collection for Hal's wife — no — that wouldn't do — you had to take that killer out and lynch him. It made all of you feel righteous and manly and it made everything a hundred times worse. Hal's wife is still down there at their house without money, without a husband, but that doesn't enter into it with men, does it? Now do you see why I have such little faith in men, Bob?"

"The Kid deserved exactly what he got, Ann."

"But why didn't you let the law do it? That's what the law is for. It would have hanged him legally, Bob, and Judge Anderson would still be alive. Why didn't you let the law work in its own way while you and the others tried to make things a little easier for Hal's family? This way you haven't solved anything, you've made it infinitely worse."

"No one knew the judge had him hidden."

"But after you found it out why did you have to *kill* him? He was an old man. Any one of you could have held him."

"He — ."

"He faced you down, didn't he? Stood up to you as a mob and that's why you shot him." She watched him grope for the cooled coffee, drink it and set the cup down. "How could you stand there and watch them kill him? He was daddy's friend and our friend after mother died."

He sprang up and went to the railing around the porch, stood with his back to her and said, "AnnaLee, I don't want to hear any more about it."

She knew he meant it. Whenever he used her full given name it was a warning. She lapsed into silence looking at his broad shoulders, the way he sagged, the

22

way he stood stooped with his hands hooked over the railing looking out into the night. She arose, took the cup and saucer, went into the house.

He was still there an hour later when the doctor and Eric Fundemeyer, owner of the Emporium, a massive, rolling-gaited man, came calling. AnnaLee took them to the darkened porch and left them.

"Have a seat," Bob said, turning, leaning on the railing watching them.

The doctor sat. Eric remained standing on wide-spread legs. His pale eyes looked moist in the shadows, his face drawn and worried.

The doctor leaned far back in the rocker looking up at Bob's face. "Bob; who shot him?"

Harrassed eyes went down to the medical man's face. "I don't know, Doctor. I don't know."

"But you were there," Eric said. "I saw you leaning against my building. I saw you pat out the fire on his coat. You knelt beside him."

"Yes," Bob said. "I suppose you saw me, Eric, but —.""

"How close were you, Bob?" The doctor asked, bright, sardonic eyes on the younger man.

"Well — as close as anyone, I guess. Doctor; I just can't remember exactly how it happened."

"Would you tell us if you could remember?"

"Certainly."

The doctor rocked a moment. "Bob; what calibre gun did you have on you this evening?"

"I didn't have one. Never carry one unless I'm travelling . . ." It trailed off. Silence closed in around them. Eric Fundemeyer's pale oval face was expression-less. The doctor stopped rocking. What AnnaLee had said came back with doubled force. "You know I don't carry a gun in town, Doc."

The doctor arose. "There's an ordinance against it, isn't there," he said. "Somebody had a gun, though." His bright glance went to Eric Fundemeyer's face. "Ready, Eric. Heard enough?"

They left and Bob Downey was slumped against the porch railing motionless, long after the street door closed behind them.

CHAPTER
TWO

He sat his horse on the hot black earth looking out at the dark sweep of land that had on its twilight depth of softness. A burly man in a faded blue shirt with tight levis, one gun around his middle with an ivory grip, a carbine butt jutting near his rein-hand, watching the sun as it went lower over the distance with a great spreading flame both blood and gold.

To the north were blue shadows falling over the burnt-dry hills. Westward lay the tang of an ancient danger that was sputtering sunlight made harsh before its stubborn retreat into the belly of the Universe.

Southward, and behind him as well, were forests, and their purple was the colour of the uplands. He had ridden out of the trees to sit transfixed; watching the land he'd been calved in.

He had no thought for the tiredness weighing on his thick, massive frame, nor for the hollow gut that quivered for food. He had no thought for the maize-yellow of the sunsplashes either. Nor for the saffron hills quick-turning and seeming to writhe in the falling light. He saw it all, it was familiar, and yet he saw none of it. Its beauty was a stirring thing; a changeless symbol of a far place, a country where cattle were king; a country cleaving unto itself with a bitter pride and a quick fierceness.

Below, far away where the last of the mountainous outfall levelled off was Holbrook, low and ugly, functional and remembered. He sat there waiting for the last of the light to die, like a solitary sentinel, his slow, black glance staying on the town. Memories flooded in greyly. The old shed behind the house where he'd hauled winter-stored fat, breathing through his mouth because of the sickening odour of rancid grease. Mixing ashes for lye into the vat, but not until the moon was right. Stirring the bubbling mass under his mother's supervision. Cutting and shaping the squares of soap afterwards.

And the fire on the stone hearth. He remembered that best. The fire and the way it made the walls glow with soft red dullness. His father's taciturnity, the squared jaw beneath the beard. The piercing black eyes, the rare smile, the might and bluntness. His mother with her expression of deep stillness. Her way of watching, of looking at a person as though she saw clean through them. Her large, long hands with the veins showing through blue and corded. Hands with a world of tenderness in them; a way of deftness that soothed and salved and saved.

He thought of others, the outfits like Cinnebar and Muleshoe and 'Gator. The times when he'd hayed with them and branded and whooped and thundered after their cattle. Of a drive — his first — to Tombstone, of running wild horses in the back country — and he waited, for the sun was still high.

26

Waited — he'd developed a knack for that. It had come hard for he'd never been a patient man, but he'd learned to wait with the years. So he sat up there on his horse seeing everything and nothing. The land was drowsy with June-warmth, summer-burnt with a crispness — and he waited.

When the shadows lengthened, drew out and made a solid blanket he started down. The way was smooth, downward swiftly over cured grass, downward to the creek east of Holbrook where the katydids made their croaking sounds and the trees were stalwart among the willows.

He paused to drink up-stream from his horse then pushed on and came into the crooked upper reaches of the stage road after full darkness was down. The town was alive. He saw men on the hard-walk, heard their calls to one another, saw the orange lamp-light lying in disturbed pools, rode through it to the southern end of town, turned off at an alley and rode into a weed-choked back-lot, dismounted, pulled a sagging shed door open and led his horse inside. The place was as dark as midnight and smelt of old things quietly rotting. The horse put his head down, rubbed ecstatically upon a smooth post while the man unsaddled him, forked him some dusty old hay, left the shed, barred the door and made his way through the weeds to the rear of the house.

Inside the same smell came to him and his spurs made the only sound. They echoed. He lit a lamp in the parlour and very slowly turned completely around. The black hearth was cold. Nothing had changed but a depth of loneliness permeated the room. He went into the kitchen, found cans of peas, meat, made a cold meal, lit a cigarette standing up, smoked it and went back outside. The lamp in the house burned steadily where no light had shown in over two months.

Overhead the purple night was balmy with myriad tiny flecks of brilliance. A scimitar-moon made watery light. He stood in the full shadows for a long time, just looking. Holbrook's residential area clustered around him. Homes and lights. Behind the walls were people. Mostly people he'd known years back. Directly across the road was Eric Fundemeyer's house. Next to Eric's was Harry Mather's place. Town Marshal Harry Mather. The black eyes lingered on Mather's place. Where had Harry been that early evening in April when they'd killed the judge? Northward four doors was Doc Harding's place. A buggy with empty shafts stood at the post before the picket fence.

He crossed the road, went through the gate at Harding's place and up onto the porch, knocked and stood back, swept his black glance up and down the roadway. Four riders loped past, the rattle and rhythm of their movement disturbing the air.

"Yes?"

He gazed at the sardonic face, the ice-chip eyes of the doctor. "Remember me, Doc?" He said.

The shadows were thick, a broad band of darkness lay across his face under the hatbrim. Doctor Harding peered out annoyed. "If someone's sick say so," he said brusquely, then the words trailed off, died, and a wall of silence settled for a moment. "Jason!"

28

"That's right."

Doctor Harding stood perfectly still. After a bit he rallied, pulled the door closed behind him and stood in the darkness looking into the square, sun-darkened face. "Over here." He moved uncertainly, threw out an arm to indicate a chair.

"Sit down, Jason."

Jason crossed to the deeper shadows but remained standing. "You know why I came back, Doc," he said. "Tell me about it."

Harding cleared his throat. "I can't tell you what you want to know," he said, "because I don't know *that* myself, but I can tell you he was dead when I got to him."

"What's rumour say?"

Harding's face resumed its sardonic expression. "Rumour! Hell — you can hear any rumour you want in Holbrook. You know that. If you don't hear it today you will tomorrow. Don't go by rumours, Jase."

"I might as well start there," Jason said. He looked thoughtfully at Tobey Harding. "You know, Doc. You've always been the one man in town that's known what's going on. Even when I was a kid you were the feller who knew the straight of things."

"This time I don't, though. Jason; if I knew I think I'd tell you. We were old friends."

"Yes, I know. Well — someone shot him, Doc. If you weren't there until afterward I reckon you've heard who was there."

Harding fell into a long silence. The same vital black eyes, he thought, the father and the son. Identical

29

square jaws, sloping cheekbones. Both were physically strong, powerful men, heavily muscled, thick-thewed, but Jason had laughter wrinkles up around his eyes, down around his mouth which was full, normally tolerant looking. The judge's mouth may have been that way once, it hadn't been for the last ten years of his life.

Harding plunged his hands into his pockets looking more morose than uncomfortable. *He's here to kill someone,* he thought. *I don't give a damn. I don't hate death; but I've got to be awfully careful what I tell him. The way he's looking at me right now he'll kill the man I name; it could be the wrong man.*

"I guess half the town saw the killing, Jase, but there's something you want to remember. Your dad was faced by perhaps four or five men. The ones behind couldn't see what was happening. Remember that because you'll hear it said that several men fired the shot that killed him. You'll even hear that more than one shot was fired and I can tell you that isn't so. One shot was fired. One shot struck your father."

"Who were the ones closest to him?"

This was the corner Tobey Harding had known he would be forced into eventually and he didn't like it. "Like I said, I didn't see him until after it was all over. He was dead and the crowd was gone."

"There was a lynching, wasn't there? What was he doing — trying to bluff them out of it?"

"The judge never bluffed, Jase. He meant what he said. Yes; as I understand it he was hiding the killer of Hal Simpson; they were out to lynch him. He refused to give him up. There was a lot of feeling in town that

30

day, I recall. This little weasel was locked up. Folks were pretty angry. I didn't think they'd go quite that far but they did. Took him out of Harry's jail and cracked Houston Mabry's skull doing it. Somehow the killer got away from the mob, ran down here. I'm not clear about how he got to the judge, but he did. The judge refused to hand him over to the lynchers."

"How many were there, Doc?"

"Oh, damned if I know. I watched from up by the stage office. They were going and coming. It was a dusty day, late in the afternoon. You couldn't tell who was in the mob and who was just trailing along for the excitement."

"But most of the town."

"A lot of them," Doctor Harding said. "But remember what I told you, Jase. Of them all only two or three saw the actual killing and there was just one bullet in him."

"Close up?"

Harding hesitated thinking back to the gaping wound. "Yes, close up. His clothing had caught fire."

Jason looked down the town. The night was hushed and serene. "Give me one name, Doc."

"No, I don't want to do that, Jase."

"How about Harry?"

"He didn't see it. I told you they took the killer away from Harry. He was knocked down and tied. So was his deputy."

"Eric?"

"No again. Eric told me he couldn't see through his window until the crowd started over to hang the killer."

Jason's black gaze was steadily unblinking on the doctor's face. He hooked thumbs in his shell-belt. "Half the town was there but you don't know who any of them were," he said flatly.

Harding's sardonic expression grew into a strong frown. "That isn't right," he said. "Listen, Jase; if I name a man it's going to start a chain reaction of trouble. You — ."

"Do you know how old he was, Doc? Fifty-eight. That's too old to be bucking a lynch-mob."

"Sure," Tobey Harding said bitterly, "and I'll tell you something else. He had no business standing up to them with a gun in his hand. He wasn't a gunman." The bright eyes, cloudy with unhappiness slewed to the other man's face. "Do you want his gun? I've got it in the house."

"Later; not right now." Jason lapsed into silence again. A strained and unpleasant silence. Then he said: "Listen to me, Doc. I'll find out — don't kid yourself about that. I'll find out, but I'd a damned sight rather hear it from you or Harry or Eric — someone I trust — than from a lot of flannelmouths. A lot of saloon bums." A flake of the hardness fell away from his voice. "It's been over two months. In that time you've heard a lot of talk, figured it out pretty well for yourself. You've got an idea who'd know — who was there — up close enough to see what happened. All I want is a name. Tell me who to talk to and I'll promise you I'll make damned sure before I do anything."

"Yeah," Doctor Harding said acidly. His gaze went southward through the night to a house he couldn't see. "And when you're finished, bring me the pieces, Jase." Then he turned and faced his visitor. "You know — if I was a governor I'd make it a law that gunmen couldn't aim lower'n the chest . . . All right. Go see Bob Downey."

"Bob," Jason said softly. "Thanks, Doc."

He went back down the walk, out through the picket gate and southward. Doctor Harding followed him as long as he could see him then listened to the soft jingle of his spurs until that, too, was absorbed by the night, then he sat down on the porch and felt around for his pipe and pouch. Resentment filled him to choking.

Downey's place was on a corner. Westerly, around from Lincoln Street, was country. Miles and miles of it that began almost before it left the fenced-in confines of the Downey property. Jason walked slowly, remembering. He'd chased AnnaLee with a whip-snake down here, once.

The door responded under his fist, swung inward and a hurrying burst of lamplight cascaded over him. He was startled to see AnnaLee like that, grown and mature, red-gold hair as thick and rich looking as autumn leaves, the heavy arched eyebrows he remembered so clearly, dark above the shock-still, gunpowder-coloured eyes.

"Jason!"

" 'Evening AnnaLee." Was four years so long? Lord; how she'd changed! " 'Bob home?"

"Come in."

He went past her into the parlour and removed his hat, held it danglingly in his left hand. Turned and looked at her again, waiting.

"I'll get him. He's out back — on the porch."

"Well," he said quickly, stopping her. "Maybe I could see him out there."

"Jason . . . ?"

"Yes."

She groped for words and couldn't find them and lamely said, "It's been quite a while, hasn't it?"

"About four years, AnnaLee."

"You knew about your mother, of course."

"Yes. I got two letters. One from Eric, one from Doc Harding. She was buried by the time they found me. That was in Montana better'n two years back."

"And you're here about — this other."

He nodded once, didn't speak.

She hesitated a moment longer then turned away from him. "Come on, Jason."

Bob Downey was smoking a cigarette. The weak moonlight made him appear heavier than he was. His face was completely expressionless when AnnaLee said, "It's Jason, Bob. Would you two like a light out here?"

"No," Bob said, staring at Jason. "I'm glad to see you, Jase. Have a chair."

Jason sat down, cradled his hat on his lap and gazed out into the murky yard, saw the rotting hen-house where he and Bob had once been caught — and lambasted — for practising roping on Mrs. Downey's layers.

"Coffee, Jason?"

34

He canted his head at her. "Well — not unless you and Bob'll have some."

She looked fleetingly, anxiously, at her brother and left the porch. Bob's cigarette was dead in his fingers. He sat hunched over looking beyond the porch railing. His voice didn't sound like it belonged to him when he spoke.

"I knew you'd be along, Jase. Figured how long it would be, would be dependent on how far off you were, when you heard."

"I was in Wyoming."

"Well . . . I don't know how to begin."

Jason's hands shaped and re-shaped the crown of his hat.

"Just tell me who did it, Bob. That's all."

"I can't. I just honestly can't, Jase."

The black eyes swung around, held to the profile of the heavier man. "What do you mean, 'you can't'?"

"I'm not sure *who* did it."

"How close were you?"

"Oh — five feet maybe. Not more than ten feet. I saw it all right — but I can't remember, exactly. I've tried, Jase. It all happened so fast. There was a lot of noise and people — ."

The black eyes didn't move. "What people? Who were they?"

Bob began rubbing his palms together. His voice gathered weight, depth, the words came faster. "Listen Jase, most of the men who were there weren't mixed up in the shooting. I know that. Like me — I didn't have a gun. All I thought of before was Hal Simpson. I wanted to see the Kid kicking up in the air for that. I didn't believe it when Jenks said the judge had him hidden in his house. I tried to make them hear me."

"Jenks Burton?"

"Yes. Jenks was there. Jenks and some of his riders. One big fellow with blond hair. I've seen him in town but I don't know his name."

AnnaLee came out with the two cups. Her brother pulled himself erect avoiding her eyes, took his cup and put it on the floor beside his chair. She said, "I don't remember, Jason; are you a cream-and-sugar man?"

"This is fine. Thanks." Jason didn't look up at her either.

She looked at her brother then down at Jason, made no move to leave and Jason gazed into the inky oiliness of the coffee, waiting for her to go. When she didn't he arose without speaking. There were just the two chairs.

An awkward silence fell. Jason was acutely conscious of her presence. Bob didn't seem to mind one way or the other. He bent, retrieved the cup and sipped it.

"Jason, he doesn't remember what happened."

The black eyes went to her face. "But he remembers that Jenks was there."

"He remembers Will Saunders being there, too," she said quickly, "and Ferris Whitley, but he doesn't remember who shot the judge."

The black eyes lingered on her face, inscrutable, cool looking, not critical just thoughtful, then they went back towards Bob. "No recollection, Bob?"

"I've tried, Jase. I can't understand it, exactly. Maybe I didn't see it. Maybe it was the shock. I kind of think it

36

was. You see, I could tell from the way things were going that the judge wasn't going to back down and those other fellers weren't either. It sort of — horrified me, thinking the judge might get shot. I was there . . ."

Jason heard the words die, the voice fade. "Yeah," he said, feeling uncomfortable, looking down into the cup again. "All right, Bob. I guess it doesn't matter too much." He whirled the dregs and watched them tumble darkly in the cup.

AnnaLee was watching him. "Why doesn't it matter?" She asked.

"Oh," Jason said quietly, "it matters. What I meant was that if Bob doesn't remember, there are others who might."

"Who, Jason?"

He leaned over and put the cup down, straightened up with his hat held in front of him with both hands, gazing at her. "Well — I go to see one man, he sends me to another. Sooner or later one them'll remember something."

"Who are you talking about?"

"This time I'm talking about Jenks Burton. Before I came here another man remembered that Bob was at the killing."

"Who remembered that?" There was quick fierceness in her tone.

Jason shook his head. " 'Doesn't matter," he said, and they exchanged a long stare. AnnaLee turned, went to the chair and sank down in it.

"Bob was among them. I'll tell you that. I'll also tell you that he didn't have a gun."

37

"He's already told me that, AnnaLee."

Her voice rang with spirit. "But maybe others have told you something different."

Jason squinted a little at her. "I didn't come here because I thought Bob did it. It would be hard for me to believe that even if it was true. You folks've always been friends of my family."

"Yes," she said. "I think there've been times when we thought more of your family than you did."

"What do you mean?"

Bob Downey looked around, pained. "AnnaLee . . ."

"I meant your mother's funeral for one thing," she said to Jason. "For another thing I meant that after your father was alone you could — ."

"AnnaLee!"

Jason said, "Let her talk, Bob."

She got up swiftly and moved in front of Jason, turned abruptly and disappeared inside the house. Bob struggled up out of his chair.

"She's upset, Jase. I guess if she *knew* what happened — if I could remember — it wouldn't be so hard on her." He shrugged looking at the still, dark face of the judge's son.

Jason waited for more to come, when it didn't he slapped his hat against his leg and said, "All right, Bob. Thanks."

Back out in the night he walked aimlessly up towards his parents' place. The noise from uptown was less strident. There was traffic in the road. A few people were fanning out along the hard-walk homeward

38

bound. Up at the liverybarn two old carriage lanterns flickered fitfully.

He sank down on the steps of his house and made a cigarette, lit it and relaxed. Funny how stories get distorted. When he'd first heard, up in Wyoming, it had been his father barricaded in the house standing off the whole town. No reason given, at least to him, by those who repeated the tale. Well; it was all coming out now. Hc could fill in thc voids without much imagination.

But Bob Downey. Of all the people in Holbrook he'd have said that Bob would have been the last to join a lynch-mob. Hal Simpson . . . Old Hal. Crinkled eyes, laughing mouth, good to kids, a great hand to tease. Well; maybe Bob'd had reason to lose his head a little. The black eyes glowed dully. And it didn't matter whether Bob remembered or not because it would all come together piece by piece and when it all fitted, all dove-tailed . . .

A big cowboy sitting slanchwise on his saddle, his hat far back and a proud set to his head was riding with two other men down the road out of town. His near boot hung free of the stirrup and when he laughed the sound rippled and boomed in the night. "Look-a-there; a light in the house." Three heads turned Jason's way. He knew they wouldn't see him. His interest sharpened; he cupped the glowing end of the cigarette, watching. But they passed on by without speaking again, their faces white blurs.

A man stepped off the far walkway angling across through the dust. The big rider looked down, said, "Howdy, Marshal." The moving shadow answered,

"Howdy," in a flat way and kept on across the road. The big cowboy followed the figure with his head, then he lifted his left hand. "Whoa. Wait a second, Marshal. You didn't sound very friendly."

One of the other riders said: "Cut it out, Nevada. Leave him be."

"Hey, Marshal; what's the matter with you; got a sore head?"

"Come on, Nevada, dammit."

"Now wait a minute . . ."

Jason saw the stooped figure, recognised it as Harry Mather's and got up off the step when the lawman came through the front gate. Behind the marshal the big cowboy was sitting crossways in the road. He didn't look or sound drunk but he acted like he was feeling feisty.

"Hey, lawman!"

Mather's figure stopped fifteen feet from Jason. The old man's head shot forward, peering. "That you, Jason?"

"Yes, it's me. Your friend's calling you, Marshal."

Mather half turned his head and grunted. "Him," he said, the word burning the air, then he started forward again. "Tobey Harding said you'd come back."

Out in the road the big cowboy had ridden back as far as the front gate. He was still sitting loose and relaxed in the saddle. "Hey — you old rack o' bone — come on back out here. When a man talks t'you civil you'd better learn some manners."

Jason dropped his cigarette. He wasn't listening to Mather. A loose-flooding anger pumped within him.

"Wait a minute, Harry," he said, starting around the marshal down across the yard toward the road.

Mather turned, half raised an arm. "Wait, Jason . . ."

The big rider saw a man approaching. He swore a little and the pale light shone off white teeth in a careless smile. "Come when y'er called. That's a good old dog." Laughter rippled.

One of the riders out in the road called out in a subdued way. "Come on, Nevada. Leave him alone."

Jason's thick figure moved fluidly down the lane. He stopped at the gate, watched the big man's smile fade, puzzlement replace it. "Are you looking for someone, mister?" he asked, features soft and shadowed looking.

"Who're you?"

"My name's Jason Anderson — what's your's?"

The cowboy's eyes widened. "Anderson," he repeated. "I asked what your's was, mister."

Nevada recovered from the surprise. Blood sang in his head, beat strongly in his body. "Anderson, huh? Well — you must be kin to the judge."

Jason brushed it aside. "Mister; I asked what your name was."

Nevada's reckless grin returned, confident and impish. "I heard you."

"Then answer."

The grin broadened. "Talkin' kind of big, cowboy. Think you can back it up?"

"Yeah; for money marbles or chalk," Jason said distinctly. "Want to get down and try me?"

The two men out in the road were listening, sitting suddenly erect and motionless.

Nevada's eyes flickered past Jason. "Evenin', Marshal," he said. "You got reinforcements, huh?"

"Go on, Wheaton," Marshal Mather said exasperatedly. "Don't start anything."

"Aw, Marshal, you know me better'n that."

"Yes," Harry Mather said. "I know you well enough. You and the rest of Cinnebar. Now go on."

Jason's glance sharpened. "Cinnebar? One of Jenks Burton's men?"

Nevada's easy glance swung back to Jason. "Yeah. You know the Cinnebar, cowboy?"

"I knew it before they had fellers like you riding for it." Black eyes swept over the big man, the way he sat his saddle, the smile he wore with its arrogance and tint of scorn. "I guess it's sort of gone downhill since I knew it, though."

"I think you're looking for trouble," Nevada said pleasantly, never losing his grin.

"No," Jason said. "I'm just waiting for you to answer my question."

"And if I don't?"

Jason's fist curled around the gate latch, springing it. In a tone as unruffled as Nevada's he said, "Why then I expect you'll get the trouble."

Nevada's grin got settled, speculative looking. He held Jason's stare with his own for a long moment, then he sighed. "Not a very friendly town, is it?" Without turning his head he called to the men out in the road. "Hey; come over here a second fellers. I've got a regular holy-terror by the tail."

Without a sound the Cinnebar men reined over beside Nevada. They looked solemn and uncomfortable. Both of them appraised Jason. One grunted under his breath at Nevada. "Let's go — dammit."

But Nevada dismounted in a graceful flourish and held up his reins. "Here; hold these a minute. This won't take long." The rider bent, took the reins, scowling.

Harry Mather was behind Jason, standing sideways a little. Now he came around with a gun in his hand. "Nevada — you get back on that horse and get to hell out of town. Go on now, I'm not kidding."

Nevada's glance flickered from the gun to the marshal's face. "He's your friend, Marshal, not mine. If he wants to get his face rubbed in the dirt why'n't you let him?"

Jason went through the gate and let it swing-to behind him. In the stillness he could hear Mather's breathing, gusty and laboured. "Shed the gun, Cinnebar."

"No!" Mather was moving closer. He cocked the gun in his hand. "Now you get on that horse, Nevada. This is the last time I'm going to tell you. Go on; by God I'll take the three of you down and lock you up."

One of the mounted men swore sulphurously. "Nevada — by God if you don't get astride we're goin' off an' leave you."

Jason watched the big man. His grin looked strained and he made no move towards unbuckling his shell-belt. "Well; make up your mind, Cinnebar. Cut or run."

Nevada laughed. He looked more rueful than belligerent. "I hate to disappoint you, Anderson, but it's four to one. I don't want to spend the night in the old man's jailhouse." He turned without another glance at Jason, took his reins, swung them around the horse's neck and sprang up. "Anyway — you never got your answer, did you?"

Jason didn't reply. He watched them turn and lope down the road into darkness. Nevada Wheaton let off a loud laugh and a ringing whoop that boomed in the night.

"Jason; he ain't worth it."

Jason turned, regarded the marshal steadily and thought that four years had worked more changes in Harry Mather than anyone else he'd seen from the old days. He lifted his shoulders and let them fall. "I guess I'm coiled for striking, Harry. It was sort of silly, wasn't it?"

"Let's go up on the porch. I see the light and Doc told me you were back."

They eased down and Marshal Mather dropped a clanger. "That was one of them, Jase. Nevada Wheaton. I didn't recognize the other two but Nevada was the one got into the judge's house from around in back and found the Verde River Kid an' drug him out. That's when the fight started."

Jason blew out a long breath. A burst of anger beat behind his eyes but he said nothing. Of course; Bob had mentioned a big blond Cinnebar rider.

"There's ten versions of the shooting. Seems like either Nevada Wheaton or Will Saunders or Jenks

Burton did it. Whoever you ask's got a different story." Mather shook his head. "I wasn't there. They tied me'n Houston Mabry up. Houston's been my deputy for about two years now. Whoever crowned him cracked his skull, too. He's only been up and around this last week."

"How about Bob Downey?"

Mather's face twisted a little on that. His answer came slow. "Well — some say he was one of them. I mean one of them that shot. Neither me nor Doc believe that. First off, Bob obeys the town ordinance about carrying firearms 'thin city limits. Second place, Bob and your dad were like father and son. Even if he'd had a gun he wouldn't have — I know it as well as I know I'm sitting here."

"Jenks Burton, Will Saunders, and this Nevada Wheaton. Who else?"

"Oh hell — you can hear anything. My wife said someone told her at the church doings that Eric done it through the window of his store. Why; that window's been broke in the centre like that for three years that I know of. I reckon if you listened long enough you could even hear that *I* did it."

Jason made a cigarette, lit it and exhaled. "I'm surprised Will Saunders is still around. I thought he'd have been gone long ago."

"He's got a horse ranch up in the Willow Creek country. Sort of a rock-stumble ranch. Not more'n three hundred acres upland and maybe sixty acres of dry-farm hay land."

"He was starting out riding for the big outfits when I left."

"That didn't last long. Will's lazy. He's been in a little trouble, too, here and there."

"Well," Jason said heavily, "what's the law done about it, Harry?"

Another long pause then: "We buried your dad a couple of days after it happened — ."

"Up on the hill?"

"Yeah. Next to your mother. Since then I've been sort of handicapped. Until Houston got back on his feet I wasn't able to do much more'n keep the drunks around town, in hand. Last week I went around asking questions. That's when I ran into the first trouble. If the boys didn't balk on me they named everyone but the Lord Almighty as the one who fired the shot." Mather fell into a long silence.

"But you're satisfied it was Jenks or Will or this Nevada Wheaton?"

"Noooo; not exactly. I got to include Bob even if it pains me to do it, Jase."

"All right. Those four then, including Bob."

"I suppose so — but dammit, Jase — that's not much to go on."

"What else do you want?"

"I *want* a confession but of course that's out. Next thing I want is for Bob to tell me what he saw. I know Bob won't lie."

"He told me he doesn't remember what happened."

"Yeah; that's what he's told all of us. I wondered for a while but Doc says it's very possible that the shock of

46

seeing the judge killed may have just kind of pulled a blind down over his mind. He said he's seen that happen with people before."

"Did he say they *ever* remember?"

"Yes. He said someday it'll clear up for Bob. That's what I've been sort of holding off for." Mather looked over at Jason. "Sure; I could arrest Jenks and Will and Nevada — even Bob — and lock them up, but I'd have to let them out again. There just isn't anything good enough yet to hold them on. Suspicion of murder's the best I can find in the book and it's got more loopholes than an old blanket."

Jason smoked and thought: *You're old, Harry. You sound tired and run-down and sort of futile, sort of defeated.*

"You want 'em arrested on suspicion, Jase?"

His answer came sharply. "No."

Harry squirmed in his chair, scowled down at his hands. "I don't exactly know whether to call in — ."

"Don't call in anyone, Harry," Jason said in the same sharp way.

"There's another thing, too. I'm quitting. I told Eric and Doc that. They're the town councilmen — your dad was the third member. Anyway, I've had enough. I'm up in years, Jase. Six years older'n your dad was. We used to joke about that. Sixty-four. That's too old for a marshal."

The voice droned on and on and Jason heard it without heeding it. He remembered Will Saunders well enough. Lanky, always a little overbearing, a little truculent. And Jenks Burton; Jenks had given him a job when he'd first struck out following the chuck wagons. Jenks . . . Nevada Wheaton. Of them all he could find nothing in his heart to remember about Wheaton. He stood up.

"It's been a long ride, Harry. I'm going to turn in. Good night."

"Good night, Jase."

CHAPTER
THREE

He rode out of Holbrook early. The full soft mist of dawn hadn't yet dissolved. The going was westward until the sun was up in full glory then he swung northward on a well-worn brace of wagon tracks as wriggley as two blind snakes and the range spread out all around him, an ocean of grass.

He sat perfectly still on a rolling ridge and let the nostalgia from deep within his remembering blood come up. Below and westward was Cinnebar. The buildings were clustered on the south side of brawling, winter-fed Cougar Creek. Across the stream was a great expanse of hay-meadow waving softly where footsteps of an invisible wind strode past.

The buildings were worn but true, unpainted, bonegrey but sturdy enough to last for centuries. The corrals had horses in them, some seeking shade, others sopping up brilliant sunlight. Three riders were making off in a northerly direction. They were small with distance, dark moving objects no larger than flies.

He went down off the slope and struck out straight as an arrow for the buildings. Several little groups of cattle were in the rushes and willows along the creek. He smelt them before they heard him coming, pushed out white faces to peer, motionless, watching to see whether he was after them or not. A big old bull was phlegmatically hooking tender willows in the downward curl of his horns, then walking forward until he'd bent the saplings low enough, then he'd stand there eating the leaves and watching the rider, doing neither with much spirit.

Jason came into the yard from behind the main house, turned and rode to the rail, stepped down, looped one rein and went up onto the porch. It was ten degrees cooler out of the sunblast. He rolled knuckles over the door and waited, looking around, remembering when he'd been a first-time-out kid, proud as a peacock; a Cinnebar rider. Jenks had been a pretty good boss, too. That made him a little regretful now, thinking back.

"Yeah?"

He turned. The man was standing out in the middle of the yard looking up towards him. He'd evidently been down by the barn. It was Jenks. Without answering Jason walked out towards him, watching the weather-darkened face, seeing it older, harder than it had been years back.

"Howdy, Jenks."

Burton made a small grunt. His expression didn't change although it must have been a surprise, seeing Jason after four years. "Howdy, Jason."

"Kind of hot out here in the sun," Jason said, stopping close to Burton, feeling the rancher's hostility without seeing visible signs of it.

"Yeah. Well — I'm busier'n hell right now, Jason."

50

"I'm not here for a visit, Jenks."

Burton's mouth closed down firmly. He stood a moment in silence then squinted his eyes a little. "All right. What's on your mind?"

Jason felt himself growing antagonistic. "I guess you can figure it out, Jenks. About the judge."

"Oh. I don't know much about that, Jason."

The black eyes grew perfectly still. "That's funny, Jenks, because everyone I've talked to said you were right up there among 'em. Even said you were the leader — the one who did the baiting."

"Who said that?"

"Who said what doesn't matter. What I want to know is who fired the shot that killed him."

Burton was quiet a moment then he said: "If you've heard all the rest you've probably heard that already — and it's probably just as much bull as folks saying I baited the judge."

Jason hooked his thumbs in his belt. His voice was quietly patient, even soft, but each word had snap to it. "It's too hot to argue, Jenks. I want a name, that's all. Who killed him?"

"Then what?" Jenks said. "You'll start a damned war."

"Won't be much of a one, I don't expect. Most folks are against killings like that. You ought to know that — should've known it before you got tangled up in this."

A little pulse began to beat sturdily at Burton's temple. His squint grew more pronounced, the eyes behind it more unfriendly, cold. "Listen, Jason; the Kid had it coming to him. I'm not sorry about that at all. If you'd been here you'd of felt the same way."

"Maybe. I'm not interested in the man who killed Hal Simpson and you know it, Jenks. Why don't you cut this short?"

"All right," Burton said swiftly. "I don't know who killed the judge. 'That answer you?"

Jason didn't answer. He was thoughtfully quiet a while. "Jenks; I know what you're doing. You want to protect a man. Well — not this time. I'm going to tell you something. If I have to yank the slack out of half the folks around here I'm going to find out who killed the judge. I don't want trouble with you unless I've got to have it, but I don't like you horsing me around, either."

"Go ask the fellers in town," Burton said turning away, lips tight, expression bleak.

Jason said, "Hold it, Jenks."

"Hold it yourself." Jenks kept on walking.

Jason's anger flooded up. He took four large strides and caught Burton by the arm, swung him violently around. They were very close and Jason's voice was pitched low and vibrant. "I meant it when I said no one was going to horse me around, Jenks."

Burton's nostrils distended, his jaw set craggily, he was silent.

"What's his name?"

Burton remained erect, motionless, grimly silent.

In a very quiet way Jason said, "I can get it out of you, Jenks."

52

Finally Burton spoke. "Try it. Just act like you're going to try it. You're a long way from Holbrook, Jason. There are two men down in the barn who'll come a-running. Go ahead — make your play."

"All right. Maybe this *is* a poor place. Maybe I wouldn't get what I want, Jenks, but you won't always be on your own ground either. If you make me, I'll dog you day and night. Make it easy on yourself. Who killed him?"

"I told you — I don't remember!"

"'Know what I think, Jenks? I think you're a goddamned liar!"

Jenks wagged his head from side to side. "You've tried all the ways and you've got nothing. Now go try somewhere else, Jason." He moved, turned fully away and started towards the barn back stiff in fiery anger. Jason watched him go, made no move to stop him and when Burton disappeared Jason went back to his horse, swung up and rode easterly out of the yard and across the range. When he got back by the sloping ridge he skirted it, hauled up, swung down and made a cigarette. Then the waiting began.

He had no plan, just patience. He had a possible advantage over Jenks Burton, though; he knew the big cowboy Nevada Wheaton, had been in at the killing. Just how valuable that knowledge was he didn't know.

He didn't expect Jenks to ride out, exactly, but he thought it likely that Wheaton might ride in if he wasn't one of the two men in the barn. And maybe Jenks himself would try to go somewhere; he knew now that Jason was back in the country, and why. He'd also know the killer — and if it wasn't Jenks himself — he'd probably try to warn him. All in all, he smoked and hunkered under the burning sun like an Indian, black eyes alert, unwavering, not content to wait but perfectly willing to do so.

The usual directness of his thoughts, unembellished, unswerving, were interrupted by a vision as he squatted in the tangled grass. AnnaLee. The strong arching of her eyebrows, the gamut of emotion that showed in her smoky eyes, the full, heavy richness of lips that lay closed without pressure and the fullness of her. It was all vivid in his mind. He had remembered her, when he'd thought of her at all in the highroads and alleyways of his wandering years, as a tawny-eyed, high-spirited, leggy girl who had looked upon him with distaste even they'd been friends, such interludes being very brief periods when he had been planning new ways to devil her, and when she had been sparring, figuratively circling, watching for the next assault.

The spirit was still there. He had noticed that the night before on the porch, the way she'd flown at him over Bob, but the spitting-cat wariness, the deep, abiding distrust of him was gone.

He reckoned her age. Guessed it around twenty or maybe nineteen. Didn't associate female maturity with the teens or the twenties and thought she looked older, an indeterminate age that was marked by maturity not years — and pretty. Not just prettiness of features and colouring altogether, but beauty of person coupled with pride of being. It was an elusive, difficult thing for him to put his mind to defining. He gave it up, watching the shimmering land from beneath his hatbrim, and thinking only that she was altogether different than she'd once been.

And Bob had changed too, but it had always been evident that her brother would be fleshy in early manhood, stout in later age, probably with a great quivering gut sagging over his belt by the time he was fifty.

Fifty brought another thought. His father had been fifty-eight. He could imagine how he had looked the evening they'd killed him, for he was durable and uncompromising. Legs wide, chin-whiskers jutting, black eyes like unrelenting rock. Jason had seen him sit in judgment on others when he'd looked like that. He could imagine him standing up to the lynch-mob just as clearly as though he had been there himself. The only thing he had trouble picturing was the faces in front of the judge. Of them all he could fill in only a few; Jenks Burton, Bob Downey, that big Cinnebar cowboy, Nevada Wheaton and — oh yes — Will Saunders.

Which one?

The sun sank. A long banner of mauve appeared in the east. On the side of the knoll where he waited shadows thickened, widened, but still no one left the ranch. Later, two riders appeared from a westerly direction and farther back, loosely, a third man rode apart. Jason watched them. They would pass in front of him but close to half a mile northward, if his surmise that they were the Cinnebar riders he'd seen that morning, was correct.

Nothing else moved so he made a cigarette and watched them. It was possible that one of them would be Wheaton. The suspicion grew stronger as the riders swung away from him a little heading for the Cinnebar buildings, and the lone horseman got closer. He rode with relaxed carelessness, a long romal, exaggeratedly long, trailing just short of the ground, and the man was big. Even riding a large horse he looked big. Jason watched, guessed four hundred yards separated the two riders ahead from the big man to the rear. He wondered if Wheaton had annoyed his companions like he'd done the night before. Decided that he had, for Nevada Wheaton was that type; big enough to make it stick, totally lacking in small humanities, truculent in a thoroughly confident, roughshod way, he wouldn't have many friends among the average range men.

Jason was coming up off the ground almost before the slanchwise seat, the spurred boot swinging rhythmically free of the stirrup, told him the last rider was one of the men he wanted to speak with.

He had no illusions when he mounted, reined around and rode at an intercepting angle towards the big Cinnebar rider. They'd almost tangled the night before; they probably would this afternoon. He felt for and freed the gun at his side and concentrated on the man in the dying distance.

Once, one of the other riders turned and gazed at him, reined up and craned, plotting Jason's course. Then they both rode on again, either assuming Jason was some rider who wanted to see Nevada Wheaton, or just plain not caring.

56

Wheaton saw him, of course, but made no move that Jason could detect. His hat was tilted well forward over his eyes and the swinging foot dangled. A little rag of grey smoke drifted upwards from his face and when they were close enough Jason could see the cigarette in Wheaton's mouth. Then Jason reined up.

Wheaton was within fifty feet before recognition came. His mouth puckered, he made a gusty sound and blew the cigarette away, then he shortened his reins and the reckless smile came up.

"Hullo there, Anderson. Still lookin' for an answer to your question? 'Come a hot long way t'do it."

Beyond the big man Jason could see the purpling hills ragged against the sky. He forced his attention to stay on Wheaton, who sat his horse in supreme confidence, both hands crossed on the saddlehorn.

"Well; d'you ride out here to whip me, Anderson?"

"I rode out here to ask some questions. Maybe you can answer them for me."

"Well; I'm not much of an answerer, even when I want to be — as you ought to know."

"I've been told you were with Judge Anderson the day he got killed."

"Have you? What about it? Listen; before this goes any farther — I've heard you're his son. If you're around here to stir up trouble over the killing forget it. First off, you aren't going to find out who done it. Second off, you'll end up getting hurt, Anderson."

Jason's black gaze sparkled. He almost grinned. "At least you're honest, Wheaton."

57

"Why not? I'm not scairt of you and that white butted gun. I got nothing particular against you, Anderson. Oh — you reckon yourself to be a staggy stud all right, well I do too; see? But this other — no dice, Anderson. No one's going to tell you anything, me least of all."

"I think someone will," Jason said. "I wouldn't be surprised if it was you."

Wheaton's reckless smile appeared, settled, and the blue of his eyes glinted. "That's easy settled. Just climb off your horse. 'Spose it's got to be now or then and it might as well be now." Nevada swung out and down, tugged the reins over the horse's head without looking at Jason, let them drop and turned. "What you waitin' for?"

Jason flung a long look down the land towards Cinnebar. The two riders were still going towards the buildings which were distantly, shadowedly visible. They were riding slowly and unconcernedly, not looking back. Jason dropped one split rein around his horn, looped it, dismounted with the other in his fist and walked around the head of his horse gazing at Nevada Wheaton. "You know," he said evenly, "you can save us both some sweat if you'll tell me who did the shooting."

Nevada laughed. It was a scorning, flat sound. "They won't come back — them fellers — and as for the other, Blacky, come and dig it out of me."

Jason dropped his rein and started forward. Wheaton took two steps away from his horse and waited. He didn't crouch or even lose his grin. Big hands fisted, up a little in front of him, he said, "Ol' black bull from the canebrakes," and chuckled.

Jason threw an overhand, lobbing blow and watched the smile widen. He smiled inwardly to himself, fired two walloping blows that landed short and he had Nevada solidly confident. He lowered his arms and looked up, waiting. Nevada came in slowly and relentlessly as though nothing could stop him. Jason hesitated until his estimate of the other man's reach warned him, then he weaved sideways and a whistling slam missed him by inches. At the same time he unwound a shattering blow that thudded into the taller man's chest with the impact of rock. Nevada yawed, rolled far back and his smile died. He bent forward to attack again, took a withering barrage from Jason's fists and faltered back another begrudging step, and swore.

Jason covered himself and went in closer. When Nevada shot an arrow-straight fist Jason was under it, still moving in. When another jab lashed out Jason countered it with an upflung arm and fired a strike of his own that was low. Nevada gasped, tried to curse, choked instead and gave way again. Then Jason measured each blow, threw them without any great speed but with paralysing effect, two hundred and ten pounds behind each one. Nevada lost more headway. A grazing fist swung him sideways. Jason straightened up and leaned into a murderous punch that struck Wheaton with a crunching sound. Nevada staggered, his hands fell, fingers unwound. Jason stepped around to face him, cruelly drove a terrible blast into Nevada's stomach and the larger man crumpled. It was under the ear where the numbing blow had landed. The flesh was purpling, swelling.

Jason watched Nevada fall, twisted to look towards Cinnebar. The two riders had vanished. Long, wafting shadows were down over the buildings. There wasn't a man in sight. He looked at his fists; one had a gouge from a button. He flexed his hands and gazed at the sprawled heap, saw it stir. With a forward swoop he took Nevada's gun, popped out the shells, replaced the weapon in Wheaton's holster and drew in a big lungful, expelled it.

"Get up, Cinnebar." He felt no anger which was odd for he'd never fought before when he hadn't been angry. Wheaton was something impersonal, detached, like an unbroke horse. Something to teach manners to, not to hate. "Come on; you're going to live. Get up."

Nevada sat up but didn't get up. He was sucking air in shallow draughts and sweat stood out on his forehead. He rolled his eyes upwards unbelievingly. "Jeezez," he said, then clamped his jaws quickly, muscles rippling against nausea.

Jason made a cigarette, lit it and bent with it cupped in his hands, towards Wheaton. "Settle your guts," he said.

Nevada brushed it aside and used both hands to push against the ground. He was white-faced when he finally stood. White-faced and glassy-eyed. He didn't try to straighten up but went to his horse bent over.

Jason watched him struggle up across the saddle and sit there with a twisted look of agonising pain. He went up to the horse's head and put a hand on the beast's neck.

"This doesn't prove much, Wheaton," Jason said. "Just that you aren't the only rooster in the henyard. Now which of you was it that killed the judge?"

But he got no answer. Nevada fumbled with his reins, snugged them. His fingers fought against being fisted. With a jerk and a rowelling plunge he raked the horse. Jason was spun sideways. When he got his equilibrium back the horse was running for Cinnebar with a loose-hanging and hunched over giant clinging to his back by will-power alone. Jason swore, watching the arrow-swift animal and the rider go towards the buildings. He considered taking a shot, decided against it for several reasons, scooped up his own reins and with a feeling of vast disgust rode through the gloomy evening towards Holbrook.

The town lights were shining with their orange-golden glow when he saw them from the west, and thirst that should have tormented him under the blazing sun, now began to do so. He came out of the country into Holbrook along the trail that became Lincoln Street when it choked down to go between houses and with reins flopping, dried sweat making him sticky, he let his horse pick the way until someone called his name, then he picked up the reins and veered over beside the picket fence, knowing before he saw her, whose voice it was.

" 'Evening, AnnaLee."

"Good evening, Jason. Bob was over to see you. Harry said he saw you ride out of town early this morning. I've been sitting on the backporch watching for you. Bob and I wanted you to come over to supper."

"Supper . . ."

She was looking up at him calmly. "We'll wait while you put up your horse and clean up."

The idea had no appeal. He sought for an excuse and failed to find one. He just wasn't in the mood.

"Well?"

"I'm pretty dirty," he said.

"I said we'd wait."

"All right, AnnaLee. I'll hurry; and thanks."

He rode across the road, up the alley and into the backlot. It didn't take long to put up the horse but getting clean wasn't so simple. The baking sun had layered him with dust as well as perspiration. When he got back to Downey's he felt dirtier than he was and the meal, while very good, was a dolorous affair he was glad to terminate as soon as possible. Bob had little to say, rarely looked up at Jason, left the room as soon as the meal was over. He offered to help AnnaLee with the dishes and was astonished when she accepted.

The kitchen was a large place, he remembered it from childhood days. They talked of it, of their families, the town and people, the school, and even a little about themselves until the dishtowel was soggy-limp and AnnaLee had taken off her apron. He had a notion she was plumbing his feelings, groping to see how he'd changed with the years. She stood over by the stove looking at him. There was a warm flush in her face. The kitchen was warm. He thought her eyes were like dew-wet gunbarrels at dawn, unblinking, sombre.

"Jason; come out in the yard with me."

He went, following her. Outside there were changes, not many. The squeaky old barrel-stave swing was still there but not very trustworthy looking. She stopped by it and the quarter-moon silvered her face and figure. She looked down at her hands as though composing thoughts into words and he noticed the pinched-tightness of her blouse, the way her heart struck sharp, making rhythmic shadows. She raised her head, shot him a glance and motioned towards the swing.

He looked a little doubtful. "You sit on it," he said. "Eighty pounds isn't two-ten, AnnaLee, I doubt if it'll hold me any more."

She remained standing and said, "Jason; I don't want you to do this."

He knew what was troubling her, had sensed it. He shrugged and said nothing.

"There's something much finer you could do?"

"What?"

"Do something for Hal Simpson's wife."

"Why sure," he said, thrown off by what seemed an irrelevancy to him. "You mean give her some money?"

"She's destitute. Yes, money would help. They had three children."

That interested him. "Hal did? I didn't know that."

"Wouldn't it better if the past were left buried and the survivors were considered, Jason?"

"To your way of thinking," he said with typical forth-rightness. "But helping Hal's wife doesn't even up for the judge, does it?"

"There's another way of looking at that, too."

He swept his gaze upwards to her face. It was a wintery and unmoving regard of her. "AnnaLee; they lynched a man that deserved it, so I'm told. Did the judge deserve what *he* got?"

"Of course not. We all know that. But don't — ."

"Then where is the justice coming from, for him?"

"There's law."

He looked ironic. "Harry Mather's law?" He shook his head at her. "We both know better than that, AnnaLee."

"Then — if you avenge him — where will that leave you, Jason?"

"Right where a thousand other sons have been."

"Does that make it right?"

"As right as rain," he said firmly.

"You are very wrong, Jason. If you kill the man — *any* man — over your father's killing, it will stay with you forever."

"All right," he agreed. "Let it. I won't be doing anything I don't believe is right, AnnaLee. It won't be murder — no drygulching. A fair fight to avenge a man who died unfairly."

"The law may not think so, Jason. You run the risk of being called an outlaw."

"I run that risk," he said, and she saw that it was hopeless, turned away from him, went over where a hastily weeded sunflower patch was rank with jutting, ugly stalks, the beginnings of seed-laden heads.

He watched her, thought she looked angry and crossed to her. "AnnaLee; as well as you knew my father how can you believe his killer should be pardoned?"

Without turning her face to him she said, "I don't believe that. I believe as your father believed. That the law, not you, should avenge him." She turned and he saw the shadowings of disturbance in her eyes. "Jason; you're trying to do exactly what your father was absolutely against. Taking the law into your own hands."

"There were some things," he said slowly, "that my father and I didn't see to an eye about. This is one of them."

She moved closer to him. "Jason; if the murdered man was someone else — if your father was still alive — he'd stop you from doing this."

"Well; when the law's strong enough and fast enough to do what individuals have been doing ever since I can remember, I'll let it, AnnaLee, but in the meantime — no. Harry Mather's law isn't going to do anything, so I will."

"How can you say that? What do you — ?"

"Harry told me he was quitting last night, that's how I know."

"Jason . . ." She touched him with one hand, let it rest a moment on his arm, and her words stopped. Something charged with astonishing force suddenly held them like statues. He reached up very slowly and took her hand off his arm, held it, then pulled tentatively and she came up against him. Almost mechanically his head lowered, his mouth fell gently against hers and the strangeness became vivid, the

65

gentleness vanished, he bore down insistently upon her mouth.

Her hands went up his arms, down onto his chest. She pushed. He let her go and felt the spiralling gust of desire sear upwards through him. The soft moonlight shaded her face a pallid colour so that the darkness of her eyes, enormous, stood out. Her mouth hung heavy. A violent spasm of shock was in her expression. Without a word he spun, walked out of the garden, around the house and beyond, to the roadway.

There was a soothingness in the night air. It cooled him, doused the fires that had burnt, turned them to ashes that tumbled and blew in the tempest of confusion within him. He angled across the streak of moonwashed tan dust of the roadway towards his house, looked up and saw the black blind windows. In one of them a tiny red tip was reflected. It grew, then faded. In the back of his mind a warning clanged. He slowed his stride. The end of a cigarette. Someone was in the yard; probably waiting for him. He veered towards the hard-walk above the house with tingling flesh. Reached for the planking with his booted foot and deliberately walked past the house hoping with all his might the manoeuvre would be successful. It was. No ripping bullet came.

At the break between two buildings he cut through to the littered back-alley and went northward. Every sense was alert. Shadows, inky and stark against the sapphire sky, were unlit buildings. Store houses, carriage sheds. He stayed where the darkness was most complete, most protective. At the alley which led into his own yard he waited, watching for movement. When none came he whisked across the alley into the yard, slunk into the gloom of the shed where his horse was.

Whoever the stranger was, he was around in front keeping in the darkness. There might be others. Jason squatted low trying to find a human outline by skylining. There were none so he crept through the weeds setting one foot down carefully, then the other. In that way he made it to the edge of the house. Lower still, he brushed along the siding as far as the front wall and there he hunkered, squinting into the darkness, muffling his breathing, unable to still the thunder of his heart.

Not far a man moved his feet. The sound was crimped and stealthy but to Jason it sounded loud. He straightened up, palmed his gun, cocked it and the brittle echo fled into the hush. A sucking intake of breath came out of the darkness, spurs rang mutedly in the weeds; the man was moving, going up towards the porch steps. Jason dropped flat, thrust his head around the corner of the building and fleetingly saw a weaving silhouette make for the steps, move up them close to the edge where they wouldn't squeak, and threw up his gun just as the shadow blended into other, deeper shadows. He drew back the gun and squirmed around the edge of the house, through the green, gritty weeds and was almost panting from the effort to keep his breathing silent.

The night was unreal, uptown there wasn't a sound. As though Holbrook knew, was waiting with baited breath. A startled rat raised up with glittering black eyes, studied Jason a moment then fled with a panicked squeal. Up on the porch a board groaned and Jason twisted over fearing the drygulcher might lean over the railing, see him down there. The nerve-searing silence grew and grew. He gathered up his legs, coiled, felt with his free hand for the side of the house and dislodged a rock which rolled against a bottle, made a scratchy, high sound. A voice boomed out at him.

"Is that you, Anderson?" The tone was pinched, harsh sounding.

Jason pressed in close looking up. The voice had come from far back as though the man was against the front wall, wasn't close to the railing at all.

"Yes, it's me. Who're you? Who'd you think you'd drygulch?"

"You," the stranger said.

Jason heard another board groan and began moving, flat-bellied against the house, gun riding easily, ready in his fist. "Then come on down here and do it."

"Sure," the man said, but he didn't move.

Jason stopped inching along the house, was tempted to risk standing up but didn't do it, weighed his chances and knew at that range he made too wide a target, head and shoulders above the porch flooring. "Well; come on," he said, then: "Drygulchers've got no guts for fair fights, though. I'll come after *you*."

"Make your play," the man said, his voice strained sounding.

Jason began edging towards the corner of the house again. He would wait until he could offer the smallest target, until the side of the building would hide all but

68

one side of his face, one eye, then he'd raise up and shoot. He knew the drygulcher could hear him moving through the weeds; half hoped the man would make a rush across the porch and expose himself long enough to snap a fast shot. But the assassin apparently knew the odds would be against him if he did that. He stayed far back, waiting.

"Come on, Anderson."

"I'm coming."

The porch floor whined. The drygulcher was moving. Jason wanted to swear. His voice had placed him for the stranger, who was now moving to gain protection, too. They were very close to a climax.

Jason raised his arm blindly, aimed where he thought the man was and fired. The night broke into shreds of crimson flame and echoes. Two fast shots came slamming back. Jason heard wood splinter and flung himself towards the corner, made it, crouched and heard the hurried gustiness of his own breath. He flattened full length against the side of the house, raised his gun and thrust it out.

The man on the porch let out a fervid curse. "Back up your big talk, Anderson," he said.

Jason's black eyes sharpened. The voice had come from the same end of the porch from which he was hidden by the siding. He drew his gun back, centred it and fired blindly through the wood. No answering shot came back but the porch flooring protested creakily as the man moved again. Jason bent over, risked a peek, saw the big shadow, brought up his gun and fired. The shadow staggered, whirled and laced three shots through the siding. Jason heard the wood splinter in the gloom behind him, took long aim and fired again. The shadow went back drunkenly against the wall. Reverberation trembled through the house-front. Then the drygulcher folded over, sagged from the waist, went down and out of the darkness came a shot, the assassin's sixth. Jason hesitated.

"Anderson? Come on."

Jason's mouth parted in a crooked, bleak grin. "You're hit, mister," he said softly. "What's the hurry; you're not going anywhere — unless it's to hell."

"Not alone, Blacky."

Blacky! . . . "Is that you, Wheaton?"

"It's me all right. Scairt now?"

That time Jason chuckled aloud. "Do I shoot like it? Did I knock you silly today like I was scairt? Hell, Wheaton — I thought you were more of a man. Drygulching . . . ?"

"I owed you this."

"Like a goddamn yellow dog . . . In the night . . ."

"It didn't turn out that way and I'm not runnin'. Come on — make it or break it, Anderson."

" 'Guts running out, Wheaton? You got one gun or two?"

Nevada fired once. "Satisfied," he said. "Anderson? I'm hit; all right — if you aren't yellow come on out in the open. Let's get it over with."

Jason hefted his gun. Two shots left. He could smell burnt powder in the night air. From a long way off someone was calling out to someone else. He closed his mind against the sound.

When he left the corner of the house it was in a diagonal rush towards the porch steps. He heard a loud grunt, saw the moonlight pale over a raised gun, turned sideways as he moved bringing his own gun up. Wheaton fired and the bullet went all the way across the roadway and smashed a window in Fundemeyer's house. Tinkling glass and a muffled scream came in its wake.

Wheaton was rolling over when Jason fired. The slug tore through the porch flooring with a ripping sound. Jason was on the steps. Wheaton was twisting to get another shot but Jason was moving lightly, on the balls of his feet. The bullet blew up a spume of dust in the alley behind them. On the top step Jason drew up, pointed downward and fired. Nevada's body jerked with impact, he dropped his gun and Jason's ears rang with the thunder thrown back from the house-front and from the wild scream that crashed out of Nevada Wheaton.

Jason went closer, saw the blood, the two guns lying there. He re-loaded his gun with his mouth drawn down, nostrils flared, dropped it into the holster and knelt. The sudden silence was deafening. When he tilted Nevada he was startled to see the man's perfectly rational stare fixed dryly upon him.

"Still here, Wheaton?"

"Yeah; still here. Don't give a damn . . ."

"Wheaton — who downed the judge?"

The dry eyes began to look remote. "Your old man, wasn't it? Tough. I didn't . . . Make you feel any better?

You didn't get him. 'Never will, Anderson . . . damn the luck . . . anyhow . . ."

Jason saw him die. Heard the last bubbling breath, saw the last flutter of eyelid, the jerk of muscle. For an unknown reason he shook the body by the shoulder, felt the lumpiness, took his hand away. There was a dark smear across the front of Wheaton's shirt. Black-shiny looking. Near the thigh was another. He whistled out his breath and got to his feet, stood there with the night coming to life around him. Stepped over the body, went down the stairs to the place where mashed weeds and grass said Nevada Wheaton had begun his drygulching vigil.

Something blue-black and wet looking glistened. He toed it, a shotgun. He'd felt no pity before, now his contempt grew. Big, proud, arrogant Nevada Wheaton, a snake-belly low assassin. You could never tell by looking; it took something like a licking to show a man's colours. He stooped, picked up the scattergun, walked over to the porch railing and shoved it through. It lay near the corpse. To those who would be coming now it would be eloquent evidence of Wheaton's intention.

He went around in back by the shed and made a cigarette. Heard men's voices after a while and knew they were in the yard, moving warily, speaking low. When they were suddenly quiet he knew they'd found the body of Nevada Wheaton.

CHAPTER
FOUR

The moon came out from behind a high blue tracery of shadow, burnished the face of the lean, sardonic man who stood in front of Jason, made his dark shoulders look frosted white. Beyond him was the vertical back of the house, darkly forbidding. Around in front were voices. The slow clopping of horses drawing a wagon out on the road sounded like double heartbeats. Someone called out: "Come up the alley, Henry; we won't have to pack him so far."

"Well?" Doctor Harding said.

Jason turned his head a little to the right. There were some big old trees, dark and twisted, still against the night. "Tried to bushwhack me, Doc."

"Uh huh. It looks that way." Tobey Harding peered at the expression on Jason's face. "Never killed a man before, did you?"

"No."

"Well; you have tonight, Jason, and believe me — you'll never forget it."

Jason swung his head back, antagonised. "Is that what you hunted me up to say?"

Harding shook his head slowly. "No; wanted to know if he got you. Lord knows you two did enough shooting."

"He didn't."

"Uh huh. Well — ."

"I met him earlier, Doc, out by Cinnebar. We had a fight. I knocked him down. He was in the yard tonight when I came back from Downey's. I saw the tip of his cigarette."

"Jase," Tobey Harding said thoughtfully, cutting through the words. "You were probably justified. I imagine folks will say you were. But there's something else."

"What? Hell, Doc — he was waiting to blast me. Didn't you see that damned scattergun — two pistols?"

"Jenks," Doctor Harding said, still thoughtful and unruffled. His disillusioned gaze came up, hung to Jason's face. "Jenks won't care whether Wheaton had it coming or not, Jase. Cinnebar riders, like Cinnebar cattle and horses, are inviolate. People just don't touch them."

Jason's face relaxed, looked almost scornful. "I talked to Jenks today," he said. "As far as he and his Cinnebar are concerned — ."

"You'd better start using your head," Harding cut in. "The biggest mistake you can make now is to under-estimate Jenks' reaction to Wheaton's killing. Listen, Jase; Cinnebar's got its own law. Maybe it didn't have when you were a kid but it does now. Why do you suppose Jenks led his riders into that lynching-bee? Because Jenks believes in that kind of law. It's his kind

74

of justice. He doesn't care a whit about Harry Mather's brand of law. He proved it when he ramrodded the Verde River Kid's lynching, didn't he? All right; you've killed a Cinnebar rider tonight. When Jenks hears about that there's going to hell a-popping and you'd better grow an eye in the back of your head because Jenks'll be after you like flies after honey."

Jason got up slowly. "Thanks, Doc," he said. "I'm going to turn in. Tell Harry I'll be down to answer his questions in the morning."

He left Harding standing down by the shed, crossed through the weeds to the back of the house, entered, went to his old bedroom and undressed without bothering with a lamp.

The next morning when he'd satisfied Harry Mather about Nevada Wheaton's killing and was walking back towards home, he passed the Welton Stage & Express Company office, glanced in automatically and saw AnnaLee standing very erect, looking straight at him. She didn't speak nor move but he hesitated, then swerved and entered the little room. Bob twisted in his chair at the sound of spurs, saw Jason and watched him without nodding.

"Morning," Jason said flatly.

AnnaLee went as far as the counter, leaned upon it gazing up at him. "You weren't hurt?"

His baleful gaze lingered on her mouth before it lifted to her eyes. He shook his head. "No."

Bob said: "The word around town is that he was hiding in the yard, waiting for you."

75

"That's right." Jason's glance went to the brother. "How well did you know him, Bob?"

"Hardly at all. Just saw him around now and then."

Jason leaned on the counter across from AnnaLee. "Well; he never struck me as the bushwhacking type."

"No, me either," Bob said. He had a strained, frightened look on his face. After a moment of silence he turned back to the papers on his desk. Jason saw the beet-red colour at the back of his neck, shrugged slightly and turned back to AnnaLee. For a moment of silence their glances locked and somehow they spoke to one another without words. Jason's flesh prickled and AnnaLee flushed and turned away. "I'm glad you didn't get hurt, Jason," she said, standing sideways and looking solemnly out of the window at the dust and traffic of the road. The words sounded heartlessly cold, automatic.

He pushed off the counter looking at her profile, thinking that she looked prim. Suddenly he was ashamed that he'd kissed her the night before. Without speaking he turned and walked out of the office.

Down the hard-walk aways he met Eric Fundemeyer. The heavy, older man stopped, waited for Jason to come up. His face was pleated with worry, his pale blue eyes moist and almost sad looking; sad and harassed.

"Jason . . ."

"I'm sorry about that window, Eric. I guess no one was hurt — I — ."

"Damn the window," Fundemeyer said throatily. "It scairt my wife half out of her skin, naturally. I'm glad you came out of it all right. Listen, Jason; take my advice this once will you; get on your horse and ride, boy." Fundemeyer's voice dropped lower, became pressingly insistent, vibrant with urgency. "Jenks'll know by now. Everyone'll know . . ."

"That's what I want, Eric."

"What? What're you talking about?"

"I want the man who killed the judge to know," Jason said. "Eric; there was Bob Downey, Jenks, this Wheaton, and Will Saunders."

"No," Fundemeyer said quickly. "Not Bob. Listen, Jason; I've known Bob since he — ."

"All right. I don't believe Bob did it either — but if he can't remember who *did*, Eric, then I'm still in the dark. I've got to include them all until I find the right one; see?" Eric's mouth fell open. Jason hurried on. "Now they'll all know, won't they? Then one of them will run for it — I'm hoping, Eric. That way I'll know who the killer was." He saw the alarm in Fundemeyer's face. "It's not the best bait in the world, Eric, but it's all I've got."

"But just you, Jason. Just one man." Fundemeyer's body went loose, sagged. "You can't do it. They'll gang up on you, boy. Listen; Jenks Burton's no one to fool around with. He's got five riders — ."

"Four now."

"— They're all loyal to him. They'll work together; they always do, Jason."

"I don't like that," Jason conceded, "but I didn't expect Jenks and the others to take this sitting down." He started around Fundemeyer. "Thanks, Eric. Uh —

if you'll have the tinker put that glass back in I'll be glad to pay for it."

He went home, cared for his horse, ate a big noonday meal and lay down, slept like a log until the evening shadows were long, then went back outside and smelled the coolness coming, fed his horse again and walked slowly through the dust towards the Downey place.

AnnaLee met him on the front porch. Bob wasn't there. "Good evening, Jason."

He dropped down beside her on a chair, hooked his feet under him and didn't look at her. "I owe you an apology," he said, staring straight out into the night, hearing the homely sounds of the town. "For last night."

She answered the same way, without looking at him. "No, not an apology; an explanation. How did it happen?"

He looked around at her briefly. "Well; I did it."

"No," she said, "that isn't what I mean. I've been wondering all day — How did I come to do that, Jason? I don't like men. They're cruel. They aren't understanding. You — most of all — yet I did that."

He cleared his throat, thought back to the things they'd said, bent forward and took out a wad of old bills. "Here, AnnaLee. Give this to Hal's widow."

Their fingers touched and fire burned behind his shirt. He didn't look up at her until he was starting to lean back in the chair again. Then their eyes met, fused in a hushed, hot glance, and very abruptly she got up, holding the crumpled bills like they were a handkerchief. "I'll see that she gets them, Jason."

78

He arose also, looking down at her. "You sound like the money's medicine she's got to take, AnnaLee."

She turned towards him, pale, big-eyed. "I wasn't thinking of the money at all — but, since you've mentioned it — that's the way you gave it. Leaning over, digging it out of your pocket as though it was something casual; something you handed out to get it off your conscience."

He was struck dumb by the sudden vehemence in her tone. By the shine in her eyes and the stiffness that seemed to hold her taller, almost defiant. "No," he said slowly, softly. "I understand how you feel, AnnaLee. I know how she'll feel too — about Hal. Years back — Hal and I stole chickens together. We trapped wild horses in the back country . . ."

Her shoulders went down a little, the just of her jaw slackened. He saw her mouth quiver and in the shadowed V of her throat the pulse had lost its rhythm, was beating softly, unevenly. "Jason, I'm sorry. I didn't mean to be — nasty, like that."

Looking at her standing there like that his mind seemed separated from his voice. The words sounded a long way off, and deep. "Nothing to be sorry about, AnnaLee. And what you said before — about me being cruel, and not understanding, most of all. I don't think that's so."

In a hopeless way she said, "But it is, Jason. You killed that Cinnebar rider last night."

"I *had* to, AnnaLee, don't you understand that? He was out to ambush me — right in my own yard. He had two pistols and a shotgun. If I hadn't gotten him he'd of gotten me."

"But when you found him — knew he was there — why couldn't you have gotten your horse and ridden away?"

His black gaze grew ironic. "What good would that have done? He'd have come back even if I'd avoided him, but you can't avoid things like that, AnnaLee — you never can. And if I had ridden off, maybe next time he'd of picked a better ambushing spot. Maybe that next time I wouldn't have been able to ride away; it was just luck that I stumbled onto him before he got me, last night."

She looked straight up into his face. "Where will it end, Jason?"

"Well," he said, "I don't know, but the judge's going —."

"Whether he'd want it this way or not?"

"Yes."

As she'd done the night before, she turned away from him, but this time she went into the house and the door closing behind her sounded final. He stood a while in the darkness, barely conscious of the scent of flowers in the night, then he went down off the porch, out through the gate to the hard-walk, and uptown. The lights of a saloon caught his eyes. He entered, took up a place around the far bend of the bar, and ordered whiskey. Nevada's last words echoed in his mind: "Damn the luck — anyhow."

He drank three straight jolts and for all the effect it had on him it might as well have been sarsparilla. He shook his head at the barkeep when he tilted the bottle for the fourth re-fill.

And no matter how he and AnnaLee started out, they always ended up the same way. Fighting. Why? What was there between them that remained so solid? His father's murder? But that was, he felt, only part of it. She'd said she disliked men; they were cruel, didn't understand . . . He plunked down a silver dollar and walked back out into the night. Well; the world was cruel. Life was cruel. Nature was cruel and he'd known women at different places — what was more cruel than a woman?

"Jase?"

He turned, the brooding darkness of his thoughts mirrored on his face. It was Houston Mabry, Mather's deputy town marshal. He hadn't seen Mabry in years. They had never been close friends anyway.

"Howdy, Houston; how's the head?"

"All knit now, Doc says. Man; whoever pistol-whipped me sure laid it on." Houston was easily eighty pounds lighter than Jason, a good seven inches shorter. He had a waspish look; the kind of gauntness that went with top-notch gunmen. Now, his grey eyes clung to the larger man's face in an appraising way. "Eric's all upset. Told me'n Harry he tried to talk you into riding away, today."

"He did."

Dryly then, Mabry said, "I see you ain't gone."

"Not yet, Houston. Tell me who killed the judge and maybe I'll ride on — afterwards."

"I wasn't there, as you've more'n likely heard," Mabry said, "but I kind of think you're going to find out who did it, Jase."

"What do you mean by that?"

"Wheaton. When somebody takes on a Cinnebar rider they take on Cinnebar. If Jenks lets that go by I'll be damned, and I've a pretty good notion that Jenks knows who did that shooting."

"He told me he didn't know. Not Wheaton, I mean the judge."

The skin around Mabry's grey eyes puckered. "Yeah," he said. "What would you expect him to tell you?"

Jason went home with his thoughts, made black coffee and drank it, slouched in the lonely kitchen. When the hour was late and he remained as wide awake as he'd ever been, he got up, took down a carbine in a saddleboot from his bedroom wall, went out back and saddled his horse, swung up and rode quietly down the alley to the road, swung northward as far as Lincoln Street, and there he rode due west.

All around him was stillness and shadows. The moon was larger, canted, tilted up a little, cheerless and alone looking. Over the last house on Lincoln Street hung a great mantling darkness that tumbled in dark disarray into the road. He saw it; saw the blur of pale movement near the porch. Saw the shadow of iridescence moving swiftly across the garden, to the fence.

"Jason!"

For a moment he let his horse keep moving. The second time she called he reined obediently around, rode in close and sat there gazing down at her.

"Where are you going?"

"Riding. Why aren't you in bed, it's late."

"I couldn't sleep. It's awfully hot inside. I like to watch the moonlight from the backporch." Words that tumbled without meaning then: "Riding where?"

His dark glance was bitter. "Riding," he said. "I'm cruel — remember? I don't understand things. So I'm just going riding."

The steel-silk colour of her eyes, paled in the light, was riveted on his face. She could see the twist of his lips, the tightness of the flesh over cheekbones, the raw violence lying still in the background of his glance. "Jason — why must you always hurt people? Isn't there *anything* that can change you?"

"Change from what?" he said. "You don't know me. You don't know any man when he's riding the trail I'm on, AnnaLee, because this isn't his everyday way of living."

Although it was a sultry night she shivered. The red-gold wealth of her hair hung loose, full and rich across her shoulders, down her back. Something primitive stirred in him. His saddle creaked when he swung down. Only the fence separated them. He put his big hands on it, gripped the palings. She saw an angry devil, brazen and hot looking, in his eyes, but she didn't retreat, move away from the thin distance that was between them; weak old fence palings.

"After I left you earlier," he said flatly, "I went to a saloon and had some drinks, and thought. Then I went home and drank some coffee and thought some more. 'Want to know what I thought about, AnnaLee? You. I came to some conclusions, too. Look — ," he gripped the palings, his forearms bulged, strained, the palings broke loose. He ducked low and straightened up in front of her, in the yard. "That's what you've got to do. Break those tomfool ideas of your's. 'Know why you have 'em? Because of Bob."

"Jason . . ."

"Bob's weak," he said brutally. "He's always been weak. Oh — he's a good enough feller, not cruel or harmful, just weak, and you've mothered him and because other men weren't weak you got it into your head that they're cruel. That they don't understand. It's you, not them, that's mixed up, AnnaLee."

"You're out of — ."

"And when I kissed you and you liked it — that threw you too, didn't it? You thought you should've hated it." He shook his head at her, chest rising and falling thickly. "And I'll let you have the other barrel too," he said fiercely. "I'm in love with you, AnnaLee — Isn't that terrible? A man loving a woman; people loving each other; hateful, mean, cruel, un-understanding men loving women?"

A strange, wild light shone fully from her eyes. She raised a hand, struck him, drew back and struck him again and the soft moonlight glanced off his head when it rocked under the blows, then she dropped her hand, weaved, and he stood like stone, glaring at her.

84

"It's a strange kind of love," he said, and turned, ducked under the broken fence and reached for the reins of his horse.

She said, "Jason; wait!"

He toed into the stirrup, grasped the horn and mane.

"Wait!" She went through the broken fence, caught at him, tugged him half around so that he had to kick his foot out of the stirrup and turn.

The way she was looking at him made something loosen inside him, give way. It wasn't the same hot-burning passion he'd felt before; he had no idea what it was. *Beautiful*, he thought: *You are beautiful, AnnaLee*. Then shame came, as bitter as juniper berries. He could taste the shame. Her eyes weren't cloudy now, they were soft and as clear as the moonlight itself.

In a torrent of words she said, "All right; you're right Jason. I *want* you to be right about me — about us — but I don't want you to be killed, don't you see? How many men are you after? All of Cinnebar and those others." Colour burnt high in her cheeks, the clearness of her eyes was like ice. "There's got to be some other way. If you're killed avenging your father — what'll be left?"

"You will," he said, "and a million other people who aren't worrying."

"But *I'm* worrying, Jason, you fool!" She reached up with both hands and closed long fingers over his upper arms, held him a moment that way then moved her hands higher until they were on his shoulders, over them, then with a savage yank without gentleness she was pulling him down to her.

His arms swept up, the reins fell away. Fingers like steel encircled her waist, held her so that breathing was painful. His mouth covered her's, moved against it and the full crush of his weight, immense and as corded-hard as ironwood, leant into her, forced her to rock back, the thickness of her hair falling lower so that the moonlight shone off her brow, and below the eyes were closed beneath a long sweep of lashes. She trembled full length. He moved away, the terrible weight lessened, breath came back to her, burnt down deeply into her lungs and she felt the heat from him without opening her eyes.

"I won't say I'm sorry for *that*," he said in a husky way.

She brought her hands forward, off his shoulders to his thick throat, cupped each one under his face, cradled it, then opened her eyes. "Now do you know why I don't want you to fight them all? Now do you know . . . ?" She turned his head a little so the soft light fell across his face. "If you died — would I feel as I do now?"

"But I'm not dead. I'm a long way from it."

She wagged his head a little back and forth. "See, Jason," she said. "You *don't* understand. The ending of a life can be much kinder than this — this god-awful uncertainty — this suffering."

"Not this sudden," he said.

"Sudden? Jason — I've known; I've known all day and last night too. Why do you think I couldn't sleep

86

tonight? Why do you imagine I was afraid of you on the porch — earlier? With a woman it doesn't have to be months and years — they know, when it happens."

"I reckon," he said. "It's like something that's been dammed up for years busting loose, isn't it? Overwhelms you."

Her eyes crinkled at him, softly. "That's exactly what it's like — so don't get killed."

"I won't," he said. "But try to see my side, AnnaLee."

She inclined her head a little then raised it again. "All right, I'll try."

He left her after that. Rode westward with a tumult inside him as uncontrolled and uncontrollable as anything he'd ever known. Rode with the moon sliding down the night ahead of him, beckoning in its forsaken, lonely way, and all around him was heaven as gunbarrel-blue as her eyes, black-earth fragrance as sweet as her memory and the stillness, the long deep throb of night that was endless. He wondered what time it was, finally, and knew that it was a small hour. That dawn wouldn't be far off. That he would make Cinnebar before the sun came again, and he did. Stopped on the crest of that sloping ridge for the second time.

Down below, on the flat rangeland hung a white blanket like a feather-quilt; sifting fog as gentle as moonlight, light, scudding, drifting with the first pale streamers of dawn. Things stirred, lifted their heads or moved inanimately like the saffron clouds, small, streamer-thin, that never came farther than the horizon where the great-dazzling disc of gold hung, its red blood gushing down over the land, sparkling in the wavelets of Cougar Creek, breaking into a thousand prisms against the ageless, bone-grey old barn and lastly, dragging a light belly over the roofs of the other buildings. The bunkhouse and smithy and cooler-house, the low, gloomy home where Jenks Burton lived.

While he watched, a cigarette dangling, squatting on the curing grass beside his drowsing horse with the carbine held upright at his side, the sunlight burnt from soft-singing gold to a harsh and brassy copper; benevolence gone and malignancy in its place. A new day was born. Another cauldron of a day that shimmered and writhed and made the earth like iron, creek water tepid, men sluggish and suffering.

Distantly a triangle called men to eat. Jason felt a small pang of hunger but his mind was independent of his gut. It closed out and sealed off the nether regions. The black eyes, sloe-like, drawn inward below the swoop of hatbrim, black coals that smouldered, never left the clutch of Cinnebar's buildings. But behind them lay a raw region of ferment where memories lay naked. A thread of truth woven, silver-like, winding through them. He had been right. She had to be handled that way. Not roughly but utterly without deception; frankly and bluntly. But the passion — he hadn't expected that, exactly. Not the fierce way it had come out of her. The way she'd slapped him and later, the way she'd met pressure with pressure. The blackness of her eyes in fury, the clearness of them in want. The way her full mouth moved in frantic speech.

Fingers like steel talons digging into him. Her lips clinging, moist-warm, in the night.

He watched Cinnebar and thought back, divided in thought and action until distantly, men began to cross the yard towards the corrals, then her image dimmed.

Small figures broke near the old barn, some going towards the barn, some towards the corrals. These latter emerged directly and joined the others. Horses were caught, men bent to throw saddles up. They eased bits into mouths, tugged headstalls back, swung up. When the last man was up Jason was standing, loose-jointed, hip-shot, waiting to see if they all rode out or if one or two would stay behind. They all rode, following behind one man whom Jason thought was Jenks Burton. Disappointment lay in him as he watched them lope away north-eastward. His mind cleared after a moment. They weren't riding towards Holbrook. Piqued, he let them get a long lead then mounted and eased his horse down off the ridge, following them.

Heat danced and the Cinnebar men looked as though they were riding inches off the ground. Without making any effort to get closer, Jason kept them in sight. In the back of his mind he recalled the land they were riding into and until they topped out over the last long gradient before coming into Willow Creek country, he was puzzled. After that, however, he thought he knew. Lifted his horse into a lope and drew him down only after he was leaning into the grade up the same gradient.

Near the top he stopped, dismounted, walked ahead of his horse until he could see down the far side of the hill. Some red-tailed hawks had a huge nest of limbs and rubbish in a fir tree. They were circling above the man and horse, making their wild, eerie cry.

The Cinnebar riders were dipping low towards a willow fringed creek. Dust lay thick in their wake. He watched them plunge into the whiplashing saplings hunched over and emerge on the far side. For a while they were lost to sight then they broke clear and rode steadily westward towards a distant scatter of rough buildings, their horses in a long-legged walk.

Jason gave them plenty of time before he followed down their tracks and by the time he was twisting his own way among the creek-willows the other men were swinging down near the buildings.

He didn't follow them out into the open but stayed near the creek where concealment lay, and coolness. A swirling herd of loose horses came, heads high, tails up and out, down to the creek. He watched them, saw the dappled stallion leader make a wide cavort, shake his head in simulated wariness, then slow to a trot and duck his head to pass through the willows. Jason looped his reins and crept upstream nearer the place where the animals were drinking and pawing. Close enough, he faded into the shadows and sought brands. Circle S on the left shoulder. Satisfied, he returned to his horse, led him clear of the willows, mounted up and rode anglingly, keeping the willows between him and the distant ranch until he was too far away to be recognisable, then he pointed back for Cinnebar. A hard fact existed in his mind. Jenks Burton had gone to see Will Saunders. There would be only one reason for that; Jason. Jenks' inspiration had probably been Wheaton's killing.

He lingered over the back-trail waiting to see which way the Cinnebar would ride when it left Saunders' place. If it went towards Holbrook Jason didn't want to be there when Jenks arrived. If it was towards Cinnebar ... A thin spiralling of dust showed pale far behind him. He turned, sat still watching it. Cinnebar returning? It took half an hour to make sure. He had to risk letting them get closer to find out, but he did it. Four riders going towards Holbrook. His eyes squinted, mouth drew down. When they got to town they'd get a body, Wheaton's, if they wanted it — but not Jason Anderson's. He cut a wide circle around Cinnebar and approached the buildings from the rear. The place was as still, as silent and deserted as he thought it would be. He left his horse out of sight, went forward afoot and got all the way to the verandah that encircled the main house before he heard a man's voice. Then he froze. It was raised in a ribald song of cowboys and the wild, wild women of some town. The racket came and went, like the singer's lungs expanded and collapsed like a concertina.

Jason went up to the dininghall door, grasped the handle and pulled. Inside, the song droned much louder. He was just inside the door blocking out the sunlight, expressionless, hulking, black eyes flat and cold, when the singer came into the room, turned towards a floor-to-ceiling cooler with a big slab of raw meat in his hands, and stopped stock-still, his mouth still open but no sounds coming from it.

"Who — who the hell are *you*, mister?"

"Never mind that," Jason said. "Who else's around here besides you?"

"Ain't nobody. Rest of 'em's gone to town — leastwise that's what the boss said when they left."

"Jenks?"

The cook's face regained its mobility. His glance grew searching. "Yeah."

"What's he gone for?"

"Oh — one of our riders got killed . . ." The voice trailed off. "Who the hell are you, anyway?"

"Me?" Jason answered. "I'm the feller killed Nevada Wheaton."

The cook's face settled into a fixed look of fear. The big hunk of meat he held sagged.

"Put that in the cooler," Jason said quietly. "Go on — you're safe enough unless you get cute."

"Not me, mister," the cook said moving towards the cooler. "Not me. Them days're long behind me. I don't even *own* a gun any more."

Jason waited until the cook had stowed the meat then said, "Come on — show me where Jenks' office is."

With a nod the cook led the way through the house. It smelt musty, masculine. At a little door the cook lifted a latch and shoved inwards. "This is it, but he don't keep much money here, I can tell you that."

"This other door — what's in there?"

"He sleeps there." The searching eyes lifted. "Do you know Jenks?"

"Used to, why?"

"Well; he ain't married. Lives here alone and — ."

"He wasn't married when I knew him. Go on in; that's right. Now sit down." Jason dropped into a straight-backed, armless swivel-chair before Burton's desk, swung half around and gazed at the cook. "What's your name?"

"Obie. Obie Carlin."

"How long have you been at Cinnebar?"

"Two years."

Jason's glance went to the shelf above the desk. A full bottle of rye whiskey stood up there. He reached forward, brought the bottle down and twisted off the cap, held it out. "Here, Obie — have a drink on Jenks Burton."

"He won't like it."

"Drink it anyway. Lots of things Jenks won't like when he gets home."

Dutifully the cook took a long swig. He shuddered, water came to his eyes. "God! Raw gunpowder in that. You going to have one?"

"No. Tell me something, Obie. What time do you expect Jenks'll come home?"

"Hell; no one could tell you that for certain. Jenks' habits are about as dependable as a mule's. Comes and goes when he wants."

Jason idled. From time to time he primed Obie Carlin with Burton's whiskey. Finally he asked the question he'd used the whiskey to prime Carlin about.

"Too bad Jenks got mixed up in that judge's killing."

"Yeah," Obie said, eyes wandering over the room with cramped vision. "Too bad a lot of things happened like they did."

"What in hell'd Jenks ever kill that judge for, anyway?"

Obie blinked. "Jenks? He never killed that judge. Where'd you pick that up?"

"Around. I heard for sure that he did."

"Naw. Godalmighty; give Jenks credit for more sense'n to kill a judge."

"If he didn't do it, who did; Nevada?"

Obie shook his head. "Naw — not Nevada. He would've though. Nevada was all for it from what I've heard the others say."

"Here; might as well kill it as leave that little in the bottle."

Carlin drank, coughed, looked for a place to expectorate and settled for the dusty place between the wall and desk.

"Who killed the judge, then?"

" 'Don't know. Argghh! Holy Mary! 'Think a feller with Jenks' money'd buy something better'n that snake venom — wouldn't you?"

"Yeah. What do you mean 'don't know'?"

"That judge? You're stuck on the subject. Hell; no one ever talks about that around here. If I was you when Jenks comes you'd better not mention that around him. He's pretty touchy about it."

"Don't worry about Jenks," Jason said, then he dropped his voice. "But who the hell *did* kill the old devil, anyway?"

"I tol' you — don't know. B'sides — he's dead — ain't he? Then wha' hell's the diff'rence. Feller's dead — plenty dead. That's all counts. 'Bassid shot 'im. Bad

94

— shootin' judges. Lots trouble." Obie shook his head mournfully.

"Well," Jason said, losing hope. "Didn't you ever hear it said who was there when he got shot?"

"There? Sure; half town o' Holbrook. Know why they don't talk 'bout it? Scairt. Scairt pea-green o' Cinnebar. Scairt o' ol' Jenks hi'self. 'Know why? 'Cause Jenks knows. He knows who sho' judge. God-damned right he knows, bu' don' make mistake askin' him 'bout it. Not ol' Jenks 'cause he'll snap his riggin' if y'do." Obie slumped low in his chair. There was moisture at the outer edges of his mouth. "Ol' Jenks knows . . . Ol' Jenks knows . . ."

Jason made a cigarette, lit it and regarded the sagging, shapeless hulk of Obie Carlin with mixed feelings. A slanting shaft of sunlight on the floor had moved several feet since he'd come into Jenks' office. "He knows, does he; well, I wonder if he'll be able to remember when he comes back from Holbrook and finds me here."

"Huh?" Obie said slackly. "Sleepy . . . goddamn' sleepy . . ."

"Lie down then," Jason said, seeing how near the cook was to sagging off the chair altogether.

"Go' n'blankets."

Jason stood up, peered out of the window at the sun. It was going down. "Sure, you've got blankets," he said absently. "Just lie on your belly on the floor there and put your back over it."

He walked out of the office, went into Jenks' bedroom, stood in the doorway looking at the rumpled bed, the clothing laid out on chairs and tables, saw the gun-rack, the spare boots thrown, some muddy, up against the wall. A dresser with half opened drawers stood across from the door. Nearer were two calendars hanging side by side with scribbling around some of the dates. "Bull's wallow," he said aloud and went back to the office.

The cook was sprawled on the floor breathing heavily, in a deep and bubbling stupor.

He went around the body and rifled casually through Jenks' desk. There was nothing there but a little under-and-over derringer which he pocketed; dozens of papers shoved back against other, older papers.

He went out into the big kitchen, drank from a dipper that lay in a water bucket, searched the cooler for cooked meat, sliced some and ate it, went out onto the back verandah looking down the land where he'd left his horse. Listened to the sounds of the ranch; horses down by the barn, farther away, a long way off the bawling of a cow. He stood out there in the refreshing coolness and clean air for a long time, then, when the sun was going down, he heard what he'd been waiting so long for; the sound of riders coming.

He put the unconscious cook into an empty room, tossed the rye whiskey bottle in the open doorway of Jenks' office and just before he heard the riders creak and jingle into the yard, he found a place to hide in the unlit, gloomy old parlour.

CHAPTER
FIVE

Two men. He saw them through the window. Two slow-moving shadows in no hurry to dismount, unsaddle and turn their horses out. Inside Jason, worry grew, thoughts clashed. Where were the other two riders? Was one of these Jenks? He crouched closer to the glass, peering. One man was stocky, short, so bowlegged even the evening dusk couldn't hide it. The other man walked towards the house bent from the waist, long arms swinging. Neither of them was Jenks Burton. Disappointment moved in Jason. He hid again, waiting to hear them when they entered the kitchen. The door slammed and one of the men swore mildly.

"Where's Obie — no lights in here." In a less concerned tone the other man said, "Well — hell — light one. I'm hungrier'n a she-bear."

There were bootsteps, the ring of spurs, a long, protracted moment of silence. A soft glow of lamplight grew, slanted squarely past the door into the parlour. Jason's calves ached from crouching. He had his gun in his hand.

"Hey," the brisk voice said. "Smell that?" The other man in his same detached manner answered: "Smell what?"

"Whiskey. I'll bet Obie's skunked. Come on, let's hunt him up."

They came through the parlour doorway with monstrous shadows preceding them. Jason was like stone. When they caught the reddish reflection off the bottle lying in the office doorway the bowlegged rider blew a dry whistle. Very softly he said, "Jenks'll kill him for that."

"Well; let him. I'm hungry."

The shorter man turned, looked over the parlour and shook his head dolefully. "Oh; the damned fool. Where d'you reckon he's went to?" But the bent-over rider was moving towards the kitchen again. "Who cares?" He said shuffling away.

Jason let himself all the way down onto the floor, straightened his legs carefully, felt the tingling sensation lessen. Neither of them had been Jenks. Disappointment passed and worry came. If Jenks had stayed in town — why? To set up another ambush?

The presence of the riders in the kitchen kept him immobilised for half an hour. When they left he could hear their muffled voices out in the yard. He stood up in the gloom and followed their progress towards the bunkhouse by the tips of their cigarettes.

There was only one thing to do, return to Holbrook. He went out of the house through the kitchen, strode southward where his horse stood, mounted and rode east across the darkening range.

When the lights of Holbrook showed, steady and sparse in the blue-velvet night he stopped his horse several hundred yards out and studied the town as though for a clue to Jenks Burton's whereabouts; what Jenks was up to in the dinginess ahead. If there was an ambush he had no intention of riding into it. He couldn't imagine what else Burton could be up to. He lifted the reins, wanted a cigarette but didn't make it, and eased the horse southward so that when he entered town it wouldn't be along Lincoln Street.

The roadway was just about deserted. Riding, Jason could see people at supper through the uncovered windows. Traffic was light but horses stood heads-down, patient, at the hitching-posts. A stage was braked at the hard-walk before the Welton Company's office. People were milling around it. A thin boy with grease bucket and ladle was bending over a rear wheel. He reined as far out of the light that fell through the office door and into the roadway as he could, watching for AnnaLee. She wasn't there. Bob wasn't either. A flickering wonder touched his mind, faded, that one or the other of them wasn't on hand to see the stage loaded, started on schedule.

Farther south, just before he ran out of stores and entered the residential area, he pointed in towards a hitchrail, tied up and stepped down, studied the hard-walk both ways and crossed to the west side, passed between two buildings into an alley, went northward as far as the liverybarn, stood down in the shadows gauging the long, wide runway, saw nothing unusual and entered. He sent a hostler for his horse. Told him to cuff the animal, hay it and grain it and leave it stalled over night, then he left still following the dark alley northward. Several yard-dogs barked at his shadow. He went as far as the rear of Tobey Harding's house, turned in and scratched at the back door. A solid and shapeless cook opened the door peering out at him uncertainly.

"Call Doctor Harding to the door," he said, and waited. When the doctor came Jason jerked his head sideways. They went to a rickety grape-arbour. Harding was watching Jason with a thoughtful expression.

"Where've you been, Jase?"

"At Cinnebar laying for Jenks."

Harding grunted. "You could've saved your time. He's been in town most of the day."

"I know. Where is he now?"

Harding's old sardonic look came up. "Several of us would like to know that," he said.

Jason frowned. He was going to speak when Harding turned away. "Take a walk with me, Jase," he said.

They went down the alley to the end of it; where it debouched into Lincoln Street. Doctor Harding opened a back gate, the latch made a sharp, sere sound in the darkness. They were in the Downey yard. Jason could smell the night-scent of flowers. He reached up, hesitated, let his hand fall back. Harding went to the backdoor and knocked. There was a lot of light showing from the windows. AnnaLee opened the door and Jason was shocked at her face. Doctor Harding pushed past her with scarcely a glance.

"Jason's here, AnnaLee; I want him to see Bob."

Her glance fell on Jason's face as he came in out of the night. She seemed not to recognise him. Without speaking she turned and led them through the house to a bedroom off the parlour. Doctor Harding passed her. She stood just inside the doorway looking down. Then, Jason saw Bob. He was drained looking, bloodless, lips blue and eyes closed. The counterpane that covered him scarcely moved. Jason went closer aware of the heavy silence in the room.

Doctor Harding bent a little, took one of Bob's arms from under the counterpane, held it by the wrist, eyes on Downey's face. He lay the arm down and gazed across the bed at Jason.

"He's pretty bad off, Jase."

"What happened to him?"

A flicker of Harding's gaze, a humourless lifting of the outer edges of his lips. "He got shot," Harding said.

Jason stood motionless. Within him instinctive knowledge stirred. "Jenks?"

"Well," Tobey Harding said letting his glance slide past Jason to AnnaLee, "someone; I couldn't say whether it was Cinnebar or not. He was coming into his front yard, you see, and someone shot him. Just guessing — from the angle of the wound and all — I'd say the assassin was across the road. Over in the neighbourhood of your place, somewhere. Not necessarily *at* your place, but in that area."

"But why?" Jason asked.

AnnaLee spoke for the first time. "I think I can answer that. Bob has said right along that he couldn't remember who killed your father. After you killed that Cinnebar rider the others — whoever they are — were afraid Bob might remember. Might tell you who killed the judge."

Harding was nodding. "I think that might be it," he said. "I came to that conclusion at supper. I also came to another conclusion. This shock to Bob's system may be exactly what's needed to restore his memory." He raised a hand. "That's just a possibility, nothing definite, but I know of cases where severe shock to a man's system has jolted things out of him that he hadn't thought about in years. In fact during the war I saw quite a bit of that. It may happen here, it may not."

Jason went closer, gazed down at Bob Downey and thought he looked dead. The room was thick with silence. He raised his eyebrows at Tobey Harding, asking a wordless question. The doctor made no attempt to answer until AnnaLee had left the room, then he said, "Damned if I know, Jase. It's a pretty messy wound and he lost a lot of blood before I could get over here to tend him. It may not be too bad but I can't say. It depends mostly on the amount of blood he lost, first, and whether or not infection sets in, secondly. Just guessing I'd say he'll come out of it fine, but if he's lost more blood than I think he has, he may never come out of it."

Jason left Harding in the bedroom with his patient. He went out to the kitchen where AnnaLee was and stood there waiting, but she didn't say anything. Her face was still, solemn anxiety deep in her eyes.

"I should have figured they'd try that," he said.

"Who could have guessed, Jason?"

He crossed to a chair, said "I should have," as he dropped down astraddle of it. "If I'd been thinking straight. It was natural. The things we all know lead to

Bob. Of all the men in town who saw the judge killed Bob was the only one who didn't say he didn't know who fired the shot. In time he probably would have remembered and told me."

"You said he was weak, remember, and if he was weak he would have been like the others — afraid to tell you."

Much of Jason's energy was gone now. He sat slumped, brooding, black eyes like dry stone. He bobbed his head once without looking at her. "All right; you've got to take it out someone. Might as well be me."

"No, that isn't it at all. I don't even hate the man who shot him. I'm past that, Jason. I don't want to take it out on anyone. I just want to know how this is going to end. It isn't just the judge's killing, nor the death of that Cinnebar cowboy — nor even Bob's shooting; it's the whole thing — all of it. You, mostly. You *and* Bob and what'll be left if there's a showdown. I don't feel angry, Jason, I feel helpless."

His head lifted a little. From beneath heavy brows he looked at her. "There's going to be a showdown all right," he said with no particular emphasis, with tiredness in his voice. "And I can just about guess who was behind this shooting, too." His eyes narrowed, grew long and pensive. "And yet — it doesn't fit him, either."

"Jenks Burton?"

He heaved a rattling sigh. "Yes. But it isn't like Jenks. Not the Jenks I worked for eight years ago. He wasn't the bushwhacking type, not at all."

"Didn't you think that of the other Cinnebar rider, too?"

"Yes, but I was just plain wrong there. I didn't know Wheaton so that was snap-judgment, but I know Jenks. He's changed, sure, I saw that the day I talked to him at the ranch, but I'd stake my life that he's no bushwhacker."

"Don't do it," AnnaLee said quickly. "You might be wrong again."

He scowled at her. "Jenk'll fight and he may not like Mather's law, but he wouldn't shoot a man from the dark." Jason got up, put both big hands on the back of the chair and looked down at the floor. "I've got to find him," he said. "There's something here that jangles wrong to me."

She poured coffee into a crockery cup, took it across the kitchen and handed it to him. "Are you hungry?" He shook his head without answering, sipped the coffee and found it lukewarm. "When did you eat last?"

"At Cinnebar," he said, straightening off the chair, looking at her. "I don't feel like eating now, thanks." He swilled the coffee. "AnnaLee?"

"Yes?"

"Has Harry Mather been here?"

"Well; he and Houston Mabry were here just after the shooting. They searched all the houses across the road, went through all the yards and sheds. Houston told me they didn't find anything."

Jason put the empty cup on the table. "How about my place; did they look over there, too?"

She nodded. "There wasn't anything there."

He looked into her eyes. "Have you thought that the ambush may have been set up for me and when I didn't come along they saw Bob and let him have it instead?"

"No, I hadn't thought of that, Jason, but it doesn't sound reasonable."

"No? They tried it night before last, you know. Ambushing me."

She hesitated a moment then finally shook her head. "I don't think it happened like that — as an afterthought. I believe they shot Bob because they were afraid he might remember what he saw."

"I guess it doesn't matter," he said, starting for the door that led out into the night.

She watched him, waited until his hand was on the latch then said, "Where are you going, Jason?"

"Find Jenks; that's all I can do."

She crossed to his side. "*This* time let the law do it. Harry said he was going to get up a posse. He said he knows who he's after."

Jason stood like an oak. "Who?" he asked.

"Jenks Burton."

Jason shook his head. "I don't believe Jenks did this, AnnaLee. I just plain don't believe he's a bushwhacker."

"But it's the same thing, Jason, whether he shot Bob or had it done."

"Maybe. I guess it is," he said slowly, "but let me work this out my way."

She reached for his arm, took it and held it tightly. He saw her, vividly shaken out of his gloominess by the bite of her fingernails. Gunmetal eyes with the high-arched eyebrows and lower, the softness of her

105

complexion, the ruddiness of her mouth, full lips slack. A pain grew in the pit of his heart. Whatever was tearing at her now was also pouring an illumination into her face that heightened her beauty. He swooped low, kissed her full on the mouth and went out into the night. Behind him she stood silhouetted in the open doorway. He didn't look back.

When he found the marshal, Houston Mabry was with him in their office. They were drinking coffee and talking loudly, arguing it sounded like, until Jason's frame filled the doorway, came through it and eased the door closed, crossed to a bench and dropped down. The voices trickled down to nothing and Mather looked more pained than surprised.

"Well — 'heard about Bob?"

"I just came from there. Doc says it'll be a tight squeeze but he's pretty sure Bob'll make it."

Mabry stirred his creamed coffee with a triumphant look. "Came 'thin an ace of gutting him, though," he said.

Jason waved away the cup Houston held up towards him. "No thanks. Harry; what've you figured out about it?"

"Nothing. Absolutely nothing. Whoever did it was close to your place, though, if that's any help."

"Waiting for me, maybe?"

"Maybe. Who knows?"

"And what're you going to do about it?"

"Arrest Jenks on suspicion or general principles, or something, and get him to talk," Harry Mather said shortly. "What else can I do?"

106

"Where is he?"

"Why, out at Cinnebar, I reckon. There wasn't a Cinnebar man in town when we made the rounds after the shooting."

"I can tell you this," Jason said. "Jenks wasn't at Cinnebar at the *time* of the shooting because I was waiting for him out there. He and one rider weren't there. Two others, a little bowlegged feller and a big bent-over rider, came in, but Jenks and his other man never showed up."

"Yeah?" Houston said. "About what time was that, Jason?"

"I was there from just before noon until after sundown."

Mabry's eyebrows dropped down. He shot a puzzled look at Harry Mather. "It could have been Jenks then," he said, and Jason guessed what they'd been arguing about when he'd come in. He felt for his tobacco sack and papers, twisted up a cigarette and blew smoke downward.

"I can't imagine Jenks Burton bushwhacking someone. He isn't the drygulching type."

"That's what I've been saying," the marshal said. "Houston says any man's a bushwhacker when he's made to do it."

Jason looked over at the deputy marshal. "What would make Jenks potshoot Bob Downey?"

"Fear. You killed Nevada Wheaton and you're out to kill whoever got your dad. That might be Jenks; probably is. He'd do anything under the cussed sun to save his hide and so would I — so would you."

107

"Not bushwhack," Jason said firmly.

"All right. Maybe you wouldn't. How do you know Jenks wouldn't?"

Jason stood up and made a weary gesture with one hand. "I've known Jenks since I was a kid and I don't believe he'd bushwhack *anyone*, but we could argue about this all summer and skate on the ice and still not settle it so let's forget it for a while."

Harry Mather set his cup on the desk with a bounce. "I'll tell you what the law's going to do. It's going to make up a posse and go out to Cinnebar and arrest Jenks Burton and it's going to do it right damned now — that's what."

"Wait a minute," Jason said. "You don't have to arrest him, Harry. Just find him and make him talk. I'll go along. We could make him talk, I think."

"Fat lot of good that'll do," Mabry said dourly. "Anyway, you'd better not be along when we find him. Bad enough as it is. With you along we might wind up with a war on our hands."

Harry Mather agreed. "That's right, Jase," he said. "You hang and rattle an' when we come back we'll tell you what happened."

Jason shrugged. He didn't think they'd find Jenks at Cinnebar. It was a hunch, nothing solider. Jenks was up to something and Jason felt confident that he wasn't at Cinnebar. What annoyed him was an inability to imagine just where Jenks was. He no longer thought he was in Holbrook.

He left Mather and Houston Mabry and the spiteful sound of their voices, crossed the roadway, ducked between two buildings and headed towards home. When he was clear of the uptown buildings it was darker. For a long time he stood motionless weighing a warning that buzzed in his head, then decided to favour it and avoid the house. He turned, went back uptown, crossed the roadway and slid into the liverybarn via the rear doorway, found some meadow hay and burrowed into it and slept.

The heat was what awakened him. He pushed out of the hay, slapped at the straws and looked out back. The sun was up and climbing. He blinked at it surprised he'd slept so long. Longer than he could remember sleeping since he'd been on his own. He went out to the water-trough and sluiced off, listened to the town noises and went out onto the hard-walk. Eric was just entering his store. Down the road a democrat wagon was grinding through the yellow dust. A saloonman over by the stage office came out to the edge of the hard-walk and flung a pan of slops out into the road. Jason crossed to the east side and walked home.

The house was stuffy but cool. He cleaned up, shaved and made some breakfast. Once the clatter of horsemen took him to the window but it was only some 'Gator riders in from the range. When he finished eating he crossed the road and went down to Lincoln Street, hiked around in back of Downey's and rapped softly.

AnnaLee admitted him. She had breakfast cooking and the house smelt of coffee.

"How's Bob?"

"The same I guess. He was asleep a few minutes ago."

"But no worse."

"No," she said, pouring him a cup of coffee, "no worse. Harry was here earlier looking for you."

"I'll look him up directly." He took the cup, put it on the kitchen table and sat down next to it. "You know, AnnaLee," he said, "if they know Bob's not too bad off they might come back."

She turned slowly and looked at him. There was a jumble of emotion with fear uppermost on her face. She said nothing.

"I thought of that this morning. That's why I came over again. If they think Bob's going to pull through all right they'll have plenty of reason to think that he might talk now, after they tried to kill him, where he didn't before."

"What do you mean, 'he might talk now'; don't you think he told you the truth about not remembering who killed the judge?"

He sipped the coffee, set the cup down. "Don't be so quick to read things into words that aren't there. I don't think Bob lied about that. Anyway, the point's to protect Bob, not question his word. At least right now." He groped in his pockets, brought out the little under-and-over derringer he'd taken from Burton's office and laid it on the table.

"There. Get some bullets for that thing from Eric. It's a .41. Keep it in your pocket. If you have to use a gun when you're alone it'll get you by. But get close with it. Get right up next to whoever you aim at

110

because those things aren't very accurate." He finished off the coffee, stood up and looked over at her. "Mind I look in on Bob?"

"No, of course not. Do you want me along?"

"If you want to come," he said, starting for the doorway that led through the parlour to Downey's bedroom. She didn't follow him and when he entered the room with its scent of carbolic acid and its heavy silence, he had to get right up next to the bed and bend down to see the wounded man because AnnaLee had pulled all the blinds.

Bob Downey's eyes were open. He stared up at Jason. There was recognition in his expression. The cheeks were sunken, bloodless looking, but a faint tint of colour was in the lips. Downey's body looked hopelessly flat and lifeless under the covers.

"Howdy, Bob," Jason said. "How do you feel?"

Downey's lips moved, but barely. "Weak. Drained dry. What happened to me?"

"You got bushwhacked in your own front yard. I didn't see it but Doc Harding told me."

"Who did it?"

"No one knows, Bob. Doc told me from the way the slug hit you the drygulcher was over by my house somewhere — in that general area anyway."

"Where's sis?"

"In the kitchen," Jason said straightening up. "I'll get her."

When he went back where AnnaLee was Tobey Harding was just coming through the back door. He turned in surprise and looked at Jason. "Well; you get around don't you? How's Bob?"

"He can talk," Jason said.

Harding and AnnaLee both looked up at him quickly. Harding's face seemed to relax. "That's encouraging," he said, and started past Jason. "I'll go see him."

Jason was facing Anna Lee. He could see her breakfast on the table getting cold. She said, "Jason; Doctor Harding told me he was in a posse that went out to Cinnebar last night."

Jason looked surprised. "Doc? What's he doing riding in posses. Harry doesn't use his head sometimes. Just one doctor — ."

"Jenks wasn't at Cinnebar."

Jason checked himself. "No," he said slowly, "I had a hunch he wouldn't be. Did he say whether they found him or not?"

"No, just two riders and a drunk man."

"Uh huh. Jenks still has that other rider with him then."

"But where is he? Do you suppose he's run away?"

"I'd like to think that," Jason said. "In fact I'd sort of figured that whoever killed the judge would cut and run when they heard I'd killed Wheaton."

"That makes it Jenks then, doesn't it?"

Jason scowled. "If he'd gone alone I might think so. Why would he quit the country with one of his hands along?"

"I haven't any idea; why?"

"He wouldn't. I wouldn't and you wouldn't. When you're running for your life you travel fastest alone, you don't take someone along who might drop out and turn you in. It just stands to reason."

"Well; but if he didn't run, then where is he?"

"Cussed if I know," Jason said irritably.

"I think you have an idea, though," she said, startling him.

They looked at one another for a moment then he said, "Come on; let's see how Doc's making out with Bob."

Harding was smoking his pipe, relaxed on the chair Jason had vacated when they entered the room. Without looking up he said, "AnnaLee; fix up some beef broth for Bob will you? Best sign in the world is when a sick person is hungry." After she'd left the room Doctor Harding nodded towards another chair. "Draw it up, Jase. Bob's in pretty good shape." The sardonic eyes went to the pallid face on the bed. "Feel like talking a little, Bob?"

Downey was watching Jason. He didn't reply. Outside, in front, a heavy set of boots clumped up onto the porch, spurs ringing. They all heard the rapping and a moment later AnnaLee's tread going across the parlour. When a gruff, scratchy voice droned indistinctively Tobey Harding said: "Harry Mather." He smiled crookedly into space. "That's good. Harry'll want to sit in on this."

Jason studied Harding's face and was interrupted in it when AnnaLee brought the marshal to the sick-room doorway and left him there. Mather came in stepping softly. Harding glanced around for another chair. There wasn't one. Jason got up and pointed to his chair, went in search of another one and ran into AnnaLee in the parlour.

"Why don't you come in too?" he said. "Bob's a lot better."

"I will. As soon as the broth's ready. Take two chairs, Jason."

He did. Carried them back inside and sat on one backwards, with his arms across the back of it, chin resting on his forearm.

The marshal gazed at Downey for a long appraising moment then swung his head towards Jason. A craggy adams-apple bobbed. In sotto voice he said, "He wasn't out there. I reckon Tobey's already told you. Me'n Houston pumped two riders — the cook was gowed t'the gills — those two riders knew nothing. All we got out of them was that Jenks had told them to go back and feed the corralled stock, do the chores and wait there until he came back."

"Did they have any idea where he went?"

"Nope. Leastwise they said not." Mather's old eyes lingered on Jason's face. "Make sense out of *that*, now."

"Shouldn't be too hard," Doctor Harding cut in. "He's either left the country or gone to roundup more help for his war."

Mather snorted. "What in tarnation would he need help for; to fight Jason here? Hell's bells, he's got his own four riders, that ought to be enough odds for any man — four to one."

"You're going off half-cocked," Harding said testily. "If he was in on Bob's assassination he'd know the law might be after him. He might have even seen our posse last night."

Mather looked down at Bob with knit eyebrows. Grudgingly he said, "That's possible. All right; let's figure he's gone for help. What for? Does he think he can storm into town and get Jason?"

Harding swore exasperatedly. "Don't be so dense, Harry," he said. "Of course not. Jenks is nobody's fool. When he goes after Jason he'll have it all worked out. For instance — he'd need more than four cowboys to watch Jason's house and the town, wouldn't he? If there's going to be big trouble four men wouldn't be nearly enough."

"All right," the marshal said. "Maybe he's planning on potshooting Jason as he rides into town or out. Now tell me this, Tobey: Just where around here is he going to find four or five more men who'd hire out to fight the law, will you?"

Doctor Harding bent a withering stare at Mather. "Where? Why — dammit — any one of a number of places. Other towns, cow camps, in the back country. Where'd you get the idea gunmen fear the law, anyway?"

Jason saw the disgruntled, angry look on Harry Mather's face. The marshal looked steadily at Bob Downey. "I'm tired," he said abruptly and Jason heard the petulance in his voice. "Being up all day and all night too don't set well with me any more." With a gleam in his eye he turned on the doctor. "And you —

you'n Eric have got my resignation — when are you going to dig up my replacement."

"One thing at a time," Harding said evasively.

AnnaLee came in with the broth. None of them spoke while she and Tobey Harding fed the wounded man. Jason watched new colour glow in Bob's face, thought that he must not have lost as much blood as Doc Harding feared. AnnaLee drew back and Jason touched her arm, nodded towards the empty chair. She sat down watching her brother.

"How bad is it, Doc?" Bob finally asked, voice stronger.

"Bad enough," Harding answered. "A might more to the south and you'd have been a goner. It entered the back above your kidneys and tore some back muscles and came out just below your arm pit, Bob." Harding settled back in his chair, struck a match to his cold pipe.

"When I was first starting out," he said in a genial and conversational tone, "there used to still be some of those old Sharps .40-.90 rifles around. When you got a man hit with one of those lead bricks you took your fee out of his pocket right away because not one in a hundred ever saw another daybreak." He made a flourish with the dead match, sucked on his pipe. "These .30-.30s now — why as bad a hole as you've got would have torn a man in two in the old days, but you'll pull out of this in fine shape. Probably won't even be stove up much. Well; not for another ten years or so, anyway. After that you may get a sore back now and then. A few winter-aches."

116

"Does anyone have any idea who did it?"

Harry Mather scowled and shook his head. "Ideas, sure; like Jason's got ideas who killed his paw, but proof — none at all."

Bob's eyes wandered, searched the corners of the room and sped along the ceiling and back to the two men and the girl. In a vague way he said, "I know who did it. When I woke up just before Jase came in, I remembered who did it."

Jason looked puzzled. "Why did you ask me what happened then, Bob?"

Downey's gaze went to Jason's face, stayed there. "Not me," he said. "I don't know what happened to me. The other. The killing of Judge Anderson. I know who did that."

The room was still. Tobey Harding's pipe jutted forgotten below his sparkling stare. Harry Mather was carved of stone. AnnaLee was motionless. Only Jason moved. His head raised up inches off his arm, black eyes unblinking like the eyes of a rattler.

"Who, Bob?"

The wounded man's gaze stayed on Jason a long time. The silence grew out, it was so prolonged it became almost tangible.

"Will Saunders."

Harry Mather looked startled. Tobey Harding's pipe emitted a furious little burst of smoke. Only AnnaLee and Jason remained as they'd been before.

"Are you sure, Bob?"

"Sure. I tried to grab him; tried to spin him around. He swore at me and Jenks started to move towards him.

I think — Jenks was going to stop him from firing. It looked that way. Your father — he — raised his arm to pistol-whip Will. If he'd fired instead he'd have killed Will. They weren't more than three feet apart. Will fired. I remember that. He fired. Afterwards I patted out the flames on the judge's coat . . . They hung Verde River Kid in Widow Taney's cottonwoods, after that . . ."

AnnaLee got up abruptly and left the room. The men sat there like stone, saying nothing, letting the silence close down again. Finally Harding took the pipe out of his mouth.

"Then what the devil is the matter with Jenks?" Harry Mather asked softly. "Why's he doing everything he can to make it look like he's the killer?"

"He isn't doing it for that reason," Jason said. "Jenks was the leader. He's still the leader." He paused, looked at Tobey Harding.

The doctor's forehead wrinkled. "It's more than you're implying, Jase," he said. "A lot more. Jenks is boss. He rules the range and he's out to rule Holbrook too. Holbrook, the law, anything he can dominate. He's always been like that, just not so pronounced is all. Maybe that's what it takes to be a successful cowman, I don't know. I *do* know — and you do too, Harry — that Jenks has been changing over the years. He has become wealthy and like a lot of successful men he wants more. Not wealth particularly, but power. He deliberately led that lynch-mob because it fed his hunger for power — for leadership. He got exhilaration from leading a whole town into something. He was drunk on the fact that men were following Jenks Burton and not the law. The fact that Verde River Kid died as a result was secondary. The fact that Judge Anderson got killed was immaterial. He wanted to hold power and he held it; influenced a lot of half-wits and led them. He was drunk on power and now he's committed. He's got to make it stick even at the risk of his own life."

Into the silence that followed his last word, Tobey Harding added: "He isn't the first man who ever acted like that and he won't be the last one."

Harry Mather moved on his chair, crossed his legs. "That's all sort of treetop stuff to me, Tobey. You've been educated to look for that high faluting stuff. My education's taught me just one thing. There's a difference between right and wrong, and Jenks was wrong. Regardless of *why* he did that — led those damned fools in a lynching — it was wrong. Illegal-wrong. That's all I care about." Mather frowned. "But I'll be damned if it didn't jolt me — this talk about Will Saunders. I was sure Jenks was our man."

Jason said, "Bob; was Will on the peck or did the judge make him shoot?"

Downey's eyes clouded. "The judge stood up to the whole mob of us. He didn't tongue-lash Will any more'n he did me — or Jenks. Will was looking for trouble with the judge; that was obvious."

Mather broke in. "Jase; two years ago your dad sentenced Will to six months' labour over butchering a 'Gator steer. Last year Will got into trouble over some horses but he left the country before I could serve the papers on him. I didn't know he was back in the country until the day of the lynching. Will had no use for the judge at any time and I expect when the judge pulled that pistol, why Will just figured it was the best legal way of killing someone he hated that'd ever come his way."

Jason thought of the Circle S horse herd in the willows and the clutch of log buildings beyond Willow Creek. Irritation grew in him. Over two months ago his father had been killed and Will Saunders was over in the Willow Creek country but Harry Mather had done nothing about it. His eyes were hot, they avoided the old marshal's face, went to the floor and stayed there. In the uncomfortable silence that ensued Jason was years away remembering a lanky, rough Will Saunders. There was hard satisfaction in the knowledge that he'd never liked Will.

Bob Downey spoke: "He didn't have to kill the judge, but it wasn't murder."

Jason's eyes flashed up. "Not murder, Bob?"

"The judge had his pistol out, Jase. He had it pointed at Will."

"Bob," Jason said reprovingly. "My father was no gunman. He — ."

"How did Will know? How did any of us know? He had the gun on Will. I think the judge would have shot the first one of us who tried to go into the house after the Kid."

"That was his right."

"Defending his life was Will's right, too" Bob said huskily.

120

"But you said yourself the judge wasn't trying to shoot him."

"How did Will know what he was going to do, Jase?"

Tobey Harding interrupted. "That'll be all, Bob. No more talking." Then he stood up and looked sternly at the others. "Come on; Bob's in no shape for this."

CHAPTER
SIX

They went out into the kitchen and Harry Mather drummed on the table in awkward silence. He slid a glance at Jason then looked away. Before AnnaLee set out the coffee cups he went over by the door and said, "I'd better be getting along," and left them.

Tobey Harding stared fixedly at the cup AnnaLee had set before him. He drew in a big troubled breath and seemed to shudder when he expelled it. "Sit down, Jase."

Jason looked at AnnaLee when she handed him his cup. In an incredulous voice he said, "Did you hear what Bob said?"

She nodded and went back by the stove.

"Sit down, Jase," Doctor Harding repeated, going loose in the chair. "I had a hunch something like that was coming. When you went out to the kitchen Bob told me he remembered who shot the judge. The way he said it made me think it wasn't going to be quite the way all of us expected it to be."

"But Doc," Jason said. "The judge didn't stand a chance and you know it."

"I suppose he didn't," Harding mused aloud. "But if it had been anyone besides Will Saunders or someone

122

like him, I'd probably look at it like Bob does." He drank deeply and set the cup down, looked across the room at AnnaLee. "Strictly speaking it wasn't murder — was it?"

Jason's big hand closed around the cup. "I'm not being strict, Doc, I'm being plain. The judge was no match for Will. Everyone knew that. He had every right to have that gun, to protect his house, even to protect Hal's killer."

"You're arguing against yourself," Tobey Harding said. "You're saying the judge was legally right — which of course he was — but what you're aiming to do is absolutely against the kind of legal right your father died for."

Jason's fingers relaxed. "You sound like AnnaLee," he said.

And AnnaLee, listening, watching them both, lost a little of her colour so that the wintery glow of her eyes stood out. A tight trembling began at one corner of her mouth. "You can't stop him, Doctor," she said staring at Jason. "He wants just one thing and he'll have it. If it tears the hearts out of a dozen people he'll have it. If it's wrong and he knows it's wrong, he'll have it."

Doctor Harding's head jerked, his eyes leapt to her face. A glaze of shock, of total astonishment swept across his face. He sat a moment longer then arose struggling with his expression and cleared his throat.

"Call me if Bob needs me, AnnaLee." He turned, leaned a little and moved his empty coffee cup aimlessly, not looking at either of them. "Jason; if you've got a moment come by the house."

After he left Jason arose, stood uncertainly, dark blood scudding under his cheeks and dull anger in his mind.

"That wasn't necessary, AnnaLee."

"I suppose it wasn't. It was the truth though."

"I can't see it any other way. I can't understand how you'd feel like you do when your brother just managed to squeeze by death."

"Can't you, Jason? Because I'm not deaf to decency, that's why I feel this way. You are — you must be."

"And if Bob had died — then what?"

"I would have wanted his murderer to die also — at the hands of the law."

He started across the room. In his walk was exasperation, in his face coldness.

"Wait, Jason."

He turned. "Well?"

"I've got to have some fresh air. Will you get a rig and take me driving?"

He blinked at her. "Driving? Now; today?"

"Yes."

"You can't leave Bob, AnnaLee, you know that?"

"I'll get Mrs. Fundemeyer to come over. She offered to yesterday. Please, Jason . . ."

He thought, it's crazy but maybe she's all tensed up inside too. He said, "All right. I'll be back from the liverybarn in a little while."

"I'll be waiting."

They went driving in the shimmering heat and the buggy top did little more than avert the direct rays of the sun. She sat like a carved doll, red-gold hair freed,

124

moving a little with the movement of the rig, large, dark eyes far away and the flatness of her mouth detracting from her beauty.

Jason drove hunched over, lines through his fingers, black eyes brooding-solemn. The awkwardness lasted until he straightened up and directed the team into a dip of land where a mossy seepage spring was, hidden among tall trees. The horses stopped, fidgeted, coats sleek-dark with sweat, and tossed their heads in anticipation.

AnnaLee turned towards him. There was a white, thin ridge above her mouth.

He got down heavily, took the figure-eight hobbles so thoughtfully provided with each 'courting-rig' by the liveryman, put them on the horses, dropped the tongue and hung the bridles on the up-ended singletree. The horses hopped into the moist shade where tall grass was, nuzzled the water and fell to eating. Jason went around the off-side of the rig and held up his hand. She took it and stepped down. He led her into the deepest shade. They sat close and it was strange that the awkward silence was still with them in the quiet peacefulness.

Jason made a cigarette, tossed the match into the pool of still water below the seepage spring. He blew smoke that was leached dry as soon as the air caught it. He gravely studied the heat-wavy range. Grass was curled, curing on the stem. Eastward and high overhead a lone red-tailed hawk spun in lazy circles.

The land was scorched but serene, patiently suffering in the fury of mid-summer. He envisioned a face, much younger than it would actually be. A lantern-jawed face with small, bright eyes and a long nose that pinched down tightly at the nostrils. And AnnaLee startled him as she'd done before.

"You're thinking of Will, aren't you?"

He flipped the cigarette into the water and nodded. "Yes. AnnaLee; let's not argue." He said it simply. The drowsiness of their niche of fragrant, soft shade was seeping into him. He didn't feel like resurrecting his anger, his resolve, just then.

"I won't argue with you, Jason. I never will. All that's happened between us, so suddenly — so unpredictably — makes arguing futile. It's hopeless." Her voice faded, died away. She sat there seeing all the things he saw and thinking *I love you, Jason. God in heaven I love you. Don't break my heart with this insanity of yours.*

"Good," he said leaning back on his elbows, staring into space and at nothing. "I shouldn't expect you to understand, AnnaLee. It's something men understand and women don't — that's all."

I'll even accept that, she thought. *I'll never believe it in a hundred years, Jason, but because you want it, I'll accept it.* She ran a hand under her hair. He saw how the filtered light from the shaded trees above them plunged deeper, writhed and curled in it. Her profile was to him. A thick want came up in him, settled in his throat so words wouldn't come. Then she turned and faced him and the gunmetal colour of her eyes was soft.

"What will you do now, Jason?"

His eyes slid off her face, lost themselves darkly in the distance. "Go on hunting, I reckon, only instead of

126

Jenks, now it'll be for Will." He shifted position a little. "AnnaLee; explain something to me. Harry knows where Will's horse ranch is. Why hasn't he gone out there? It's been almost three months since the judge was killed."

"You know why as well as I do. Harry is old. He's a tired old man. When your father was killed it hurt him more than a lot of us were hurt by it. They'd been friends for thirty years, Jason."

"I'd have gone hunting his killer all the harder, then," Jason said.

"Perhaps you would have, but Harry's a different man. It sickened him, Jason. Took the spirit out of him. Made him confused and older. Instead of fighting back he resigned as marshal. For him it's the crowning defeat to a long life of strife. Can you see that?"

"I reckon," he said musingly. "I expect that's right. I just wanted someone to put it into words for me."

Looking at him steadily she said, "Is there anything else you want put into words, Jason?"

He felt the blood beat up and around his ears. His black eyes swung to her face, held there, grew warm in their stare while his mind groped for something he was afraid to touch. "Us," he managed to say. "Put that into words, AnnaLee."

"I'm not that bold, Jason." She caught her heavy underlip and held it with her teeth, looked at him. "Or am I?" Her mouth relaxed, the cloudiness left her eyes. "Yes I am but prove to me you want that put into words."

127

He pushed up off the grass, close to her. "Like this?" He said, kissing her, feeling the softness of her breath, uneven, on his upper lip. The sturdy thudding of her heart through his shirt. The heat of her, close. Then she moved her face and he bore down so that her mouth quivered under his before she turned her head sideways and refused to open her eyes or look up at him.

The palms of his hands were damp. He ran them through the cool grass, reached up for her, caught her and dragged her in against him. "AnnaLee — tell me."

She spoke with her head still sideways, eyes open now and bleakly fixed on the scruffy old cottonwood trunks nearby, twisted and gnurled with the years, the storms and tempests.

"I've lost track of right from wrong, Jason. You've made me do that, but I've discovered something else. When we were younger — when you used to chase me with snakes — I hated you, didn't I? Only it wasn't just hate because hate's got something else to it. Do you know what I'm talking about?"

He didn't answer the question, just held her so that the hard, sharp gusts of her breath beat against his chest and said, "Go on."

After a pause she said uncertainly, "I'm not exactly sure myself, but I think I was in love with you even then, Jason. When you left I used to tell Bob it was cruel of you to leave your parents like that. It wasn't your parents though, Jason, not really. It was me I was thinking about. You were being cruel to me. You hurt me terribly when you did that." Suddenly she swung to face him and their faces were inches apart.

128

"I've thought of that since last night. The things you said after I slapped you. I said you were right, then, but I didn't believe it. I only said it because I was so afraid I'd lose you again. I could stand anything but that, Jason. You could do anything to me but leave me again, Jason. Anything. I'm not strong enough to stand that." The words came faster, almost without direction or thought.

"I never could stand other men. They didn't understand and they were cruel. Jason; that was a reflection in me, of you. You'd left me and other men couldn't take your place — do you see? They were the hate I had for you because you left. Oh . . . I'm not making sense, am I?"

He took his hands off her and leaned back. "AnnaLee; when I said I was in love with you I was as surprised to hear myself say it as you were to hear it. Listen; the kind of love you've imagined is gentle and romantic, isn't it?"

"Yes."

"But I can't bring you that kind — not yet — maybe never. I'm not like Harry Mather. I can't give up that easily. I'm not like Doc Harding either, accepting everything because I think bad things have to happen in this world. I'm different from Eric and Houston and all the rest of them — different from Jenks and Will and even from the judge."

"You could change, Jason," she said.

But he shook his dark head at her. "I couldn't. If I tried to it would be a lie, AnnaLee. I couldn't keep it up. Not as long as I want to be with you; for years and years."

A scald of small tears burned in her eyes. She leaned towards him. "Jason . . ."

Her face was hot against his, her mouth pliable, full and moist. She moved against him, rolled her head a little first one way then the other way and a soft moaning, strangled words, came from her. He pulled her down and when the kiss ended he was leaning on one elbow, the black torrent of fire in his eyes naked and moving.

She drank in his face, put up one hand and traced out the ruggedness of his features. "Jason; if you get killed . . ."

He waited, saying nothing, watching her, awed by the fever and the fire.

". . . I'll die."

Within him the rich throb of blood was heavy. He wanted to reassure her but uneasiness swam through his mind. Should he give this up for the other? The eyes like dew on steel at sunrise, the strength and comfort and disquieting closeness, the incredible wealth of her company, of her being? His mind grew dry with the struggle. There was no answer; there never would be. He lifted one sleeve and ran it across his forehead where prickles of sweat lay.

"That's what I mean, AnnaLee. I love you, you know that, but the kind of love I bring you isn't moonlight and roses. The kind women want. It's a bad kind and yet if I rode away nothing would be solved."

"No."

"Because before I go this time — if I do — I've got this other to take care of first."

"Yes."

"And that wouldn't solve anything between us, would it?"

"No."

She lay passive below him with the filagree pattern of shade across her. The glow of her eyes was as stark as the smoke rising from a tipi on a wintery day. She said, "I told you I wouldn't argue with you, Jason. Say what you want, do what you want, believe what you want — I won't argue about it."

His mouth curled in a slow smile. "Well; some men might like a woman that agrees all the time but I don't."

She responded to his small grin with a soft lifting of the outer edges of her mouth and a gentle look in her eyes. "You don't have that kind of a woman. I think you know it, too. You know what I think without me saying it, like I know what you think."

He considered that, turned it over and over in his mind and decided that it was so. "Then tell me what I'm thinking right now," he said.

"That you love me."

"Wrong. I was thinking you're beautiful enough to take a man's breath away."

Her lips parted, her eyes danced at him. "Oh Jason — first you frighten me then you confuse me then you make my heart feel like it's bleeding. Why?"

"I've already told you. Because that's the kind of love I bring to you. A bad kind."

131

"I want it, good or bad. I think only little girls believe love can never come any way but under a full moon and apple blossoms, anyway."

"I think," he said, "that you've just come to that conclusion then, because a half hour ago you talked differently."

"All right. I just have. Heartache makes people grow up, doesn't it? God knows I've had my share of it the last few days." She smiled gently again. "And Jason — if you think that was a half an hour ago you're very wrong. Look up there — where the sun is now."

He looked and was bewildered. The livery horses were standing side by side, eyes closed lower lips hanging, twitching now and then. The shadows which had been almost directly overhead when they'd arrived at the seepage spring, were slantingly long and deeper. It was late afternoon. He pulled her up by the shoulders and patted at some leaves in her hair, ran his hand deep into the auburn wealth of it and closed a strong fist into a knot of bone, brought her head around and looked down into her face. She was waiting, eyes wide and hungry. He kissed her and she threw her arms around him, bruised his lips with her own, surprised him with passion as she'd done the night before under the scimitar moon. Then she pulled swiftly away and jumped up dusting at the leaves, the tendrils of dead grass that clung to her dress.

Jason got up heavily with knees turned to water and where, when he'd first sat down there had been a core of bleakness deep within him around which all other emotions lay, now there was a thrilling and hungry flame that burnt steadily, never slackening.

He put the livery animals back across the tongue, made the singletree fast and hooked the traces with fingers that only half obeyed his will, and every way he turned he could smell the scent she used.

They rode back towards Holbrook leaning back against the quilted seat, rarely speaking, both tired, emptied of emotion, almost listless. The sun cast dagger-straight sinews of blood-gold light down the land. A blind little breeze went scurrying low across the range making a sobbing sound and AnnaLee sat bolt upright for a moment, then sank back again and spoke.

"Jason; don't be reckless. Jenks is a dangerous man."

"I won't be," he said, watching the skyline of Holbrook march steadily across the range towards them. "It's Will I'm after though, not Jenks — unless he forces me."

"I don't think your trouble is going to come from Will, though. Jenks is the one who is doing the thinking in this. For Will as well as for others — himself, any of the men who might think you'd have a reason to hunt them up."

"Outside of Will I don't know who they'd be."

"That's just it, Jason. Jenks knows others witnessed the judge's killing. He's smart enough to play on that."

He turned and looked at her, baffled. "What do you mean?"

"You couldn't find him. Neither could Harry. He was in town most of yesterday but he left before Bob's shooting. You were at Cinnebar and he didn't return

133

home. I think it's very possible that Jenks was going among the other ranchers and riders who were in that lynch-mob and telling them that you were after them, too."

"But wasn't most of the mob townsmen?"

"Most of them, yes. I saw them through the door of our office. There were a lot of ranchers and riders in town that day. They were also in the mob. And Jason — why did Jenks spend so much time in town yesterday? If you'll ask questions I think you'll discover that he was frightening the townsmen, too."

Jason thought about it. Hunched over the lines and creased up his forehead and worried over it. By the time he was back at the house on Lincoln Street he felt that AnnaLee was close enough to being right to warrant looking into it. If she *was* right, at any minute a fearful townsman or rider might blast him from hiding. AnnaLee held his fingers a moment after he'd handed her down onto the hard-walk.

"Come back, Jason. Come back for supper."

"I won't promise," he said feeling the coolness, the pliability of her hand rousing his blood anew. "Golly but you're pretty."

She let go of his hand. "I'll be waiting for you."

He drove the team back to the liverybarn, paid and used the back alley to go down to Harry Mather's office. No one was there. He retraced his steps through the soft dusk to the back of Tobey Harding's place, knocked and waited. The same thick-bodied cook saw him and went for Harding without opening the door. The doctor had a searching look in his eyes when he

134

came out and led the way to his grape arbour. He turned and motioned towards a rickety bench.

"Jase; I've been thinking again." He stopped speaking and looked intently at Jason. "But first — don't get mad if I'm probing too deeply where I've got no business."

Jason looked at Harding then looked away. He said nothing.

"I got an impression this morning . . . The doctor stopped speaking and sniffed, wrinkled his nose and tested the air. Jason watched him a moment then realisation came and he burnt brick crimson. Harding looked very steadily at him, cleared his throat and began fumbling through his pockets for his pipe. "On second thought," he muttered, "maybe I'd better just avoid the topic."

Jason looked up. "Doc? AnnaLee?"

Harding nodded vigorously. "You brought her up now, remember that, so I'll put in my two bits worth." He held the pipe cupped in his hand, made no effort to fill or light it but regarded the bowl with great interest. "I got the impression this morning that she's become fond of you, Jase. Well now — suppose something happens to you before this mess is settled? Do you see what I'm driving at?"

Jason got up, moved restlessly. "I've been thinking about that most of this afternoon. It still boils down to the same thing."

"What?"

"Nothing is changed by it, Doc."

Harding fell to contemplating his pipe bowl again and the silence grew between them. Finally he got heavily to his feet and said, "Well; that doesn't leave the rest of us much of a choice, does it?"

"What do you mean, 'the rest of us'?"

"Nothing much, but I for one don't like to see a girl's heart broken and her dreams blown apart in gunsmoke." Harding pocketed his pipe. "I've seen so damned much of that senselessness, Jase. Killings. Shootings." He was silent a moment then asked if Jason had eaten. Jason thanked him, said no to the invitation.

"I just came by to find out how Bob is. Went down to Harry's office but there wasn't anyone there."

"Bob is miserable in body and spirit. He and I had a long talk this afternoon, while AnnaLee was out. He doesn't want to look at the judge's killing like he does, but on the other hand he wants to be perfectly honest with himself and you about it. You know, Jase, I've seen brooding like he's doing kill men in his shape and it's a shame."

Glumness settled over Jason. He couldn't shake it off. Bob had to feel that way, he guessed, and he appreciated his honesty, but his own feelings weren't influenced a bit.

Tobey Harding rocked back and forth watching Jason's face. "I've got an alternative if you'd care to hear it."

"Shoot, Doc."

"Well; we both know Harry's law is pretty damned ineffectual. It's too bad but there it is. Now, would you be willing to wait until Eric and I've found a suitable man to take Harry's place? I mean, would you be willing to give the law one chance to handle this affair legally, before you go after Will?"

Jason studied the ground at his feet. "This morning you told Harry 'one thing at a time' when he asked about that replacement. That means you don't have a replacement in mind, doesn't it?"

"No," Harding answered. "We've got a replacement in mind but up until a few days ago he wasn't in shape to take over the job."

The black eyes swung around. "Houston?"

"Yes."

Houston Mabry. He culled all that he knew about Mabry and filtered it slowly through his mind. Houston was aggressive all right. He was hard and realistic. Without Harry to circumvent him at every turn he might be able to buck up Holbrook's law, make it respected. He frowned in indecision and a new thought occurred. Everyone knew he was out to kill his father's killer. What would they think if he stepped aside and let the law take over? That he had suddenly lost his nerve.

"I can't, Doc. For your sake and Bob's and Anna-Lee's I wish I could, but I can't."

He left Harding standing under the dilapidated rose arbour and went home. Thoughts staggered across his mind in a limping line. He made a cold supper out of cans and ate it without tasting any of it. Made a cigarette and went into the dark parlour, fell into a chair and smoked it in the gloom until scuffing boots scraped across the front porch and a fist rolled across the door. Then he crossed to a window, peered out, grunted and went to the door and threw it open.

" 'Evening Harry."

" 'Evening Jase." The marshal stood teetering in the opening.

"Come on into the parlour; I'll light a lamp."

When the glow dissolved the darkness Harry Mather came into the room, went straight for a quilted rocker and sank down into it with a sigh.

"Been lookin' for Jenks and Will. God but it's hot out."

"Find them?"

"No but we found a dozen places they'd been."

Jason turned, leaned on a table with a tasselled cover across it. His black gaze was narrowed and intent. "What 'dozen places,' Harry?"

"Ranches, cow camps, different places they rode through today and yesterday afternoon." Mather screwed up his eyes at Jason. "Damnedest thing — now don't get me wrong, Jase — your paw's killing was bad — but I had no idea the whole cussed country's up in arms over it. Why, I even got told I ought to lock *you* up for killing that Cinnebar drygulcher. Folks're sure riled up. 'Haven't seen the beat of it since the old Indian raiding days."

Jason left the table, went over by the black hearth, made a cigarette and regarded the lawman over the smoking tip of it. Just exactly what she'd said. Almost the same words. He made a hard laugh and Harry Mather looked up at him, startled.

"What's funny?"

138

"Nothing. Remember when you and Doc were arguing over Jenks being able to hire a gun crew this morning in Bob's bedroom?"

"Yeah; what about it?"

"Well; Jenks is even smarter than *that*. He isn't going to have to hire a single gun, Harry. He's going around telling men I'm after them for being in on my father's killing. Damn him anyway — but he's smart."

Mather dropped his head, looked at the scuffed toes of his boots. "Houston said the same thing, Jase. I didn't believe it because I don't think folks'd be more scairt of you than they are of the law, and so far I've only been after one man — Jenks." The blue eyes lifted again, went to Jason's face in a pensive gaze. "See?"

"I see," Jason said. "How did they act?"

"Well, some of 'em just plain wouldn't talk at all. In fact most of 'em wouldn't. The ones that would were sweating bullets. Couple of them even said they were moving on. Doggondest thing I ever saw."

Jason half turned, tossed his cigarette into the fireplace and watched it lie there smouldering for a moment. When he turned back he said, "Harry; I'm due over at Downey's for supper."

Mather got up stiffly, flexed his legs and grunted. "I'm about wore out," he said, "and I still don't have him. Where the devil do you imagine the fool went to, Jase?"

"Cinnebar, Harry. I'll bet you a fat heifer he's at Cinnebar right now — tonight."

Mather stood still, staring. "Why would he go back there? By now he knows the law's looking for him."

"And by now," Jason said, "he's ready for the law. He's got the countryside stirred up, half the men in town ready to fight too, unless I'm guessing wide, so he's home resting a little. Waiting to see what will happen next."

But Mather shook his head when he started for the door. "Nope," he grumbled. "I don't believe it. I believe he's hiding out somewhere."

Jason closed the door behind the marshal and went into the kitchen, ladled water into the wooden sink and began his ablutions. While he cleaned up and dressed in fresh clothing he thought of Jenks Burton and Will Saunders — and Harry Mather. Always two steps and a holler behind everything that happened, poor old Harry.

He was met at the door by AnnaLee. She had on a creamy coloured dress that fitted well. So well in fact he got caught staring and smiled foolishly and she blushed.

"Go in and visit with Bob until I call you."

He went, the ghost of his smile lingering, a lightness in his heart he'd never felt before. An almost giddy lightness. Bob was pushing a large bowl aside when Jason entered. His gaze went quickly to the black eyes in a questioning glance.

"Howdy, Bob."

"Howdy. I didn't think you'd want to breathe the same air I do, Jase."

Jason sat down. It was hard not to feel pity. It was harder to banish the vision of AnnaLee in the cream coloured dress. What Tobey Harding had said came

140

back to him. He repeated it to Downey, then shrugged. "You think what you want, Bob. I'll think what I want."

"I'm sorry, Jase."

"No need to be. Men've thought differently before and gotten along."

"I reckon," Bob said, and lapsed into silence a moment. "Jase; has anybody figured out who shot me yet?"

"No. Harry was over at my placc a little while ago and he didn't mention it. He's been hunting Jenks all day and didn't find him, which shouldn't surprise him."

"Do you think Jenks did it?"

Jason's gaze clouded briefly. "I don't think so, Bob. Others probably do but I just can't picture Jenks as a drygulcher."

"No," Bob said perplexedly. "Me either. Then it had to be Will Saunders, didn't it?"

"Not exactly. Jenks has been stirring folks up. He's got everybody who was in the lynch-mob thinking I'm gunning for them. It might have been one of them who shot you. Some fool who was afraid you'd say they killed the judge."

"But that doesn't make sense, Jase."

"Being in a lynch-mob to start with doesn't make sense but it makes as much sense as thinking Jenks potshot you."

Bob lay back staring upwards. "AnnaLee thinks they might come back to finish the job. Look in that drawer there; she got a belly-gun somewhere and put it in there for me. Silly little .41 under-and-over thing."

"I know," Jason said. "I gave it to her."

Bob's head rolled on the pillow. "Do you think they might come back?"

"I don't know but we ought to be prepared. One thing is sure-fire, Bob. If Jenks and Will knew that you remembered who killed the judge and told me, I wouldn't want to put any money down on how long they'd let you live for doing that."

Bob's face looked sunkenly worried. "Well — Lord — isn't there something better than that pea-shooter around here?"

"I'll get you a better gun," Jason said rising, hearing AnnaLee's steps approaching beyond the bedroom door.

"Thanks," Bob said, then, like Tobey Harding, he got an odd look on his face when AnnaLee came to the doorway. He looked from Jason's shining face and clean clothes to his sister's sparkling eyes and creamy dress. "Say Jason," he said. " 'You staying for supper?" Jason nodded as colour mounted under his tan and the black eyes moved uncomfortably. Beyond him AnnaLee was watching her brother. She finally plucked at Jason's sleeve, he bobbed his head at the wounded man and left the room. Downey watched them go with a startled expression across his face.

They ate in the kitchen and AnnaLee alternated between looking at him steadily for moments on end and avoiding his eyes for equally long moments. Jason had been hungry, now he wasn't. AnnaLee watched him pick at his steak and pie and creamed potatoes with bewilderment.

"Aren't you hungry, Jason?"

He looked solemnly down at the food. "I was, yes'm, but somehow I'm not now. But it's good. It's the best I've tasted in almost five years."

"Then eat it," she said practically. "I don't like having people come to supper and play with their food."

He ate. The more he worked at it the easier it became until he was satiated and his plate was empty.

"You can smoke," she said. "Bob always does after supper. My father did, too."

He smoked and drank coffee and felt almost at peace with himself and the world. The lamplight got tangled in her hair, swept severely back and caught in a long tumbling mass by a ribbon. The way the light careened when she moved her head made him think of the way the sunlight and shadows had splashed over her at the seepage spring.

"I'll help you with the dishes."

They were standing, looking at one another the length of the table. "No," she said. "Not this time, Jason. Let them; we'll go out on the back porch while you finish your cigarette."

He followed her out into the soft darkness with its fragrance of flowers and, heavier, more constant, the earthy smell of the range, the curing grass, the baked earth. He pinched the cigarette to death between his fingers and tossed it aside. "I'm through with it," he said standing near, perfectly straight.

She whirled and went into his arms, her mouth seeking his, her long fingers gripping his upper arms,

143

creeping over his shoulders and working at the bulge of his back muscles.

"Jason! Jason!"

"I want to marry you, AnnaLee. Want to — hell — I've *got* to!"

She opened her eyes and stared at him. A quick-running flame burnt fervently in the background of her eyes. "I didn't know *men* ever had to get married," she said. Then a shocked look slid over her face. "I ought to be ashamed — oughtn't I?"

"Never"

"When do you *have* to marry me?"

"Now. This minute. Tonight. No later than tomorrow. Will you?"

Her voice was stronger and calmer with him than it had been all day. "Of course," she said, lying close to him. "It should be soon, too, because this isn't easy for me — moments like this."

"You're not alone," he said gruffly, sliding his arms around her waist, feeling the sturdiness of her, the solidness of her body and the warmth.

"I shouldn't let you kiss me any more. Especially now — tonight. Nor hold me or touch me — until we're married." She closed her eyes as his grip tightened. "But I will, Jason. I will."

A sudden and insistent thundering on the back door brought them both around with a start. AnnaLee sagged, gasped, put a hand to her face. Between the fingers she whispered, "You go, Jason. Oh God! The last time it was Bob . . . I'm afraid."

144

He took her by the shoulders, forced her down into a chair and bent low, brushed his lips across her mouth, up across her temple and into her hair, then hurried through the house with only the crashing of his own bootsteps beating louder than the blood in his head or the clamouring fist that was shattering the night and raining blows upon the door.

"All right, dammit, just a minute." He groped at the latch, fought it free and swung the door inward. Tobey Harding was standing there for once shorn of his aplomb.

"Jason! I've looked all over town for you. Should have come here first, of course. Was upset, I guess."

"Well; come in. Don't stand in the doorway with the light shining on you like that. If you aren't skittish about things like that I am."

Harding entered. Jason closed the door and turned with a frown. "What the devil's wrong with you, anyway?"

"Harry rode out to Cinnebar alone, tonight."

"Oh?" Jason's frown stayed up. "I probably put that bee in his bonnet. He was over at my place right after he got back to town. We talked about where Jenks was. I told him I'd bet Jenks was relaxing out at Cinnebar. He must've gone out there right after that."

"Why he went isn't important," Tobey Harding said. "He went. He didn't even tell Houston he was going."

"Well; he doesn't have to tell Houston everything does he?"

"No, but if he'd taken Houston along and maybe a few more he'd be all right now."

Jason's heart constricted like a rawhide band was shrinking around it. "What's the matter with him, Doc?"

"He got shot."

Jason's hand felt for his shell-belt. The thumb hooked itself there and his black eyes were as still as the dark night outside. "Who shot him? How do you know he got shot?"

"A Cinnebar rider, short, bowlegged fellow, brought him in tied across his horse. He's unconscious."

"Not dead?"

"No."

"Can he talk?"

"Not yet. I've got him sleeping under morphine."

"All right, Doc," Jason said flatly. "Just a minute. I'll get my hat. We'll go see him."

"He may sleep for hours yet, Jase."

But Jason was gone, sweeping through the house with his big stride. AnnaLee was waiting, small, cowed, on the porch. When he swung through the doorway she stood up to face him.

"I heard, Jason. I won't keep you."

He touched her face, saw the way the late moon cast a silvery shadow over a thin wet line down her cheek. There wasn't anything to say; he couldn't think of anything. Cold, calculating fierceness made his eyes blacker than midnight. He brushed her mouth with his lips. "I'll be back, darling. I'll be back. I love you . . ."

146

She heard the tremble go through the house as he went back towards the kitchen then the back door slammed and faintly, while she watched, a bear of a man trailed by a thinner, shorter man, hurried down the lane to the alley gate and out of it. The darkness swallowed them but she didn't move until the last footfall was gone, then she felt for a porch upright with one hand, her head dropped and a tearing shiver ran through her.

"God . . . Please. Don't let anything happen to him. In my lifetime I've had three men to love. My father my brother — and Jason. You've taken one, almost took another one — please — let this one come back to me, Father."

The moon was thicker, stronger. It rode high overhead in its eerie sea of moist light, alone and aloof.

CHAPTER
SEVEN

Tobey Harding stood over the waxen face in a bleakly watching way. Jason took in the parchment skin, the skein of wrinkles like erosion gouges worn into some sidehill throughout antiquity and Harry Mather's age was uppermost in his mind. Harry looked as frail-old as some of the grey-etched biblical figures he'd seen in a book once. Old beyond expectation or right.

"Where's the wound, Doc?"

"Low, through the right hip, slanting upwards like he was on his horse when he got it."

Jason dropped his glance again. Under the white coverlet a thin old body lay lifeless. He looked around for a chair, found one and sank down. A strange fury was rising up in him. "They didn't have to shoot an old man like Harry. Hell; they could've just run him off."

"Yes, and he was alone too."

"He looks pretty bad, Doc."

"I suppose," Tobey Harding said frankly, "that he'll die. Old people die easily. I've heard a hundred lectures in my lifetime, Jase, given by medical men who ought to know. They say oldsters're fragile, their bodies worn out, their resistance low. I don't believe that's what makes 'em die — like Harry here. I believe it's

148

something medicine hasn't found yet. A thing called spirit — soul. They're old, yes, but it isn't age that makes them die easily, it's their melancholy, their mental weariness. The things they've known and believed in are gone. Their friends are gone. In this case your dad, in other cases old companions, relatives. They see that strife never ends, that good never triumphs. That for every evil overcome ten more rear up, and they get to seeing the whole thing — life — as a hopeless battle against impossible odds. They're tired of it, Jase. Just plain tired to death of it."

Jason's black eyes went slowly to Harding's face, stayed there a long time in utter silence, then he spoke. "Doc; why would Harry die? Because of how he feels about things or because he got shot, lost a lot of blood?"

"Well — the loss of blood is bad, but it's more than that, like I just said. I believe he'll die; I'm pretty sure he will, Jase, but he won't die just yet. Not while he's unconscious or doped up or asleep. He'll die after he awakens and remembers all that happened — not just his own shooting but all the rest of this goddamned tangled, murderous mess. That's what'll suck away the last of his resistance; the futility of bucking something he can't beat — life."

Jason got up, looked down at the grey face, older than any face he could remember seeing. "I don't believe that," he said. "Not altogether, Doc. I think that he's just too old for all the riding and whatnot he's been doing. I think he shouldn't have to keep on being a lawman in his sundown years. It's hard enough on a young man."

Harding's sardonic expression came up. "It amounts to the same thing," he said.

Jase shrugged. "All right; it's getting too deep for me only I don't want Harry to die." He said it with soft and simple directness. "You keep him going, Doc, I'm going after Houston."

"And?" The doctor asked standing across the nearly lifeless form on the bed.

"And get a posse."

"I see," Harding said. "More business for me."

A little sharply Jason said, "How else?"

But Harding was past caring. He made a little gesture with one hand, waving Jason away. "Oh Christ," he said, "I don't care — kill 'em all — get it over with."

Jason's black gaze hung on Harding a moment then he shifted his stance, looked at Mather thoughtfully and said, "What'd happen if you brought him out of his sleep?"

"I couldn't, I don't think. 'Gave him enough to knock out a horse. I wanted him to sleep deeper than the shock he was in when that man brought him here."

Jason said, "I don't think I'd better wait."

Harding dug out his pipe and popped it into his mouth unfilled, unlighted. "There are ways — but shock on top of shock would very likely kill him, you see."

"Yeah. All right, Doc. You keep him perking until I'm back."

150

He left Harding's house with a leaden heart and a resolve oddly unencumbered with any kind of passion. No great burning anger, no fierceness at all. When he found Houston Mabry the deputy was hurrying towards the residential district with grunting Eric Fundemeyer in tow. They both stopped at sight of Jason, waited until he came up and looked into his face. Mabry said, "You seen Harry?"

"Yes; he's down at Doc's so full of dope there's no telling when he can talk."

Mabry swore. Fundemeyer's thick shoulders drooped, his eyes fell away, went down the night towards Harding's house. He said nothing.

"He came from Cinnebar," Jason said, "and that's my fault. I told him earlier this evening I thought Jenks would be home now."

"Cinnebar . . ."

"So let's make up a posse, Houston, and go out there. What Harry can't tell us I'm pretty certain Jenks can."

"Yeah," Houston said slowly. "Cinnebar first and Willow Creek second. Jenks or Will — they'll know." The deputy's small, sharp eyes glowed. "I'll get the riders — meet you at the office directly."

Jason watched them move away and now the first stirrings of excitement moved within him. He went back to the liverybarn got his horse, saddled up and rode slowly down through the soft, warm darkness, heard the hum of voices around him in the night, saw dark silhouettes as men gathered by the marshal's office, some a-horseback, more afoot, others ambling

151

up, the raised inflections of their words coming distantly, interestedly, questioningly. Slowly, like a roused beehive, Holbrook underwent a sluggish change. The word of Mather's shooting, the raising of an avenging posse, was going around. Horsemen sat in front of the office looking at one another and the ground, the buildings, the sky, saying little. Armament bristled, faces shone white and anxious. Jason said nothing. He heard Houston Mabry's scratchy voice and watched the deputy ride towards them counting aloud.

"Six, seven, eight — nine. You make ten, Jase." He reined up beside the larger man. "Ten's enough. I picked 'em. Didn't want any doubtfuls and that sort of hamstrung me, in a way, 'cause there's lots of the boys I'd like to take, except they — ."

"I understand. Ten. Well; let's go."

As though to reassure himself Mabry looked around at Jason. "Cinnebar?"

"First," Jason said, turning his horse, putting slack in his reins and letting the animal pick his own gait down the road.

People watched them go and except for a few unsuppressed tipplers hardly a word was sent after them. The town lay in deeper darkness than the night, buildings square, functional and ugly, except where stingy streamers of light spilled, making orange vividness. Here and there the splashes of light showed a spray of brown or sorrel or grey where horsemen were, and the impersonal gleam of guns, spurs, bits.

A prickly-heat sensation ran under his skin when the silent posse turned west on Lincoln Street. She would

152

know, would probably be watching, see them. It made him extremely uncomfortable. Cause her more heartache. Oh, damn. But this was compromise, too. He was letting the law do it, only he was going along so that negated it. It wasn't altogether that she wanted the judge's killer handled by the law though, it was probably more to the point that she just didn't want him killed. He didn't look at the house but tilted his head a little and studied the high overhead.

What would have happened if he hadn't come back? Hadn't heard of his father's killing, or if his father hadn't been killed? She would have wound up like old Miss Tomlinson, a neighbour they'd once had when he'd been a kid, probably. Withered and testy, disagreeable in a complex and frustrated way. Been a schoolma'm maybe, like Miss Tomlinson, with all her beauty spoilt by some mysterious drying-up of inner juices, like acid, making people uncomfortable but especially making men uneasy in her presence.

It wouldn't happen though. But why hadn't he thought of her before; or had he? Had there been a kernel in his heart like had been in her's through the years? He didn't know, was uncertain about that but knew he'd never forgotten her if he hadn't thought of her much in his wanderings. There was a difference though. Memory is unreliable. It left her indelibly unchanged while actually four years had made such drastic changes. He'd been startled when she'd first faced him in the Downey doorway. Now, no matter what happened, she would always be a vivid picture in his mind. No matter what happened . . .

"Nice night."

He looked at the man on his right, nearly as big as he was, riding easily but awkwardly, as though the years had robbed him of a once-known familiarity with the saddle.

"Eric. You shouldn't be along, you with a family and all.

"No," Fundemeyer said, "I suppose I shouldn't. I mean — all the rest of it considered — I shouldn't, but there's more to it than that, too. You know?"

"Yeah, I know."

"The judge, Harry, maybe you . . . I risk my neck so I can look myself in the shaving mirror every morning."

They rode slowly. There was no great hurry. Houston Mabry and one or two others were alert, sharp-eyed and moving through the night with their minds projected ahead, to what they might face — would face — but most of the men were slack in the saddle, smoking peacefully, enjoying the blessing of a warm, beautiful summer night. There was a little talk, strings of words that drifted behind as they forged steadily ahead. Over them and with them rode a sort of fatalistic awareness that trouble lay at the end of their trail, but trouble was no stranger, they had been teethed on it. All they'd ever asked was fair odds. Now they had them.

Mabry spoke suddenly, riding stirrup with Jason. "Reckon we ought to try and surround the place? Jenks might have the other stockmen around the country all keyed-up to resist. Might get a rider away while we're there. We don't want a damned war if we can help it."

154

"Be pretty hard to do with ten men, Houston, Cinnebar's pretty big."

"I know. What I was thinking — sort of like the Army does — put vedettes around the place but out a ways on the range, see? They'd hear anyone riding out."

Jason looked steadily into the darkness. Jenks wouldn't run from Holbrook's law. He might laugh at it or shoot at it but he wouldn't run from it. "It won't make much difference," he said. "If you want, put out-riders around the buildings."

Houston threw Jason a quick look. "Won't make much difference," he said. "The hell it won't. I got this figured differently than Harry had it. I think Jenks' got about half the country set against the law. It's like walking on eggs as far as I'm concerned."

Jason looked around at him. "Details," he said. "Houston; I want to ride in alone, first."

Eric Fundemeyer interrupted. "They shot Harry, Jason," he said.

"Yeah. Well; it's night now. Chances are they'll miss me. I want them to try it anyway. Just one shot."

"Huh!" Houston grunted. "What makes you think they'll only fire one?"

Jason didn't answer. They rode along in silence for a half an hour then Jason reined up and the possemen piled up behind him. Eric was craning his head forward. Houston bit off a corner of plug tobacco, tongued it up into his cheek, rolled his jaws and spat. "Jase?"

"Yes. Listen, Houston — I'm going to ride down into the yard and yell for Jenks. If you fellers'll kind of keep an eye open . . ."

"All right. Eric and I'll stay out here but I want the rest of the boys to scatter out and prevent anyone from leaving."

"Fair enough," Jason said lifting his reins. As an afterthought he said, "When you fire — if you do — remember where I am."

"Sure."

Eric said nothing. His eyes followed the departing figure with concern. He twisted in the saddle heavily. "Houston; be sure and tell your men where he's going. Damn; I don't like this."

"You think I do? Bullheaded cuss." Houston turned his horse and rode among the possemen.

Jason felt as he had before. Not anger, no need for hurry, just an undeviating resolve, a calm dedication to something. He eased his gun in and out of its holster twice and when the lights of Cinnebar showed his glance quickened, became sharper, keener.

Far off was a vague drift of spiney mountaintops black against the night. Closer were eerie lifts of land soft-purple in the gloom. There was a smell of cattle, horses, the clean scent of cookstove smoke. As his mind catalogued each smell and sound he remembered back, how the same things had stirred him when he'd been a Cinnebar rider. And Jenks. Better not to think of those days. But Jenks Burton had been different then. Or had he? No, probably not. The difference was in Jason himself. In time, more than anything. Jenks had been

156

just cresting the wave of success his years of labour had brought. A first-time-out kid could worship a Jenks Burton in those days because the older man tossed him a bone of a kind word then. The kid was nobody, nothing, so he rated the figurative pat on the head and he'd worshipped Jenks.

Now the kid was a man and Jenks had engineered the death of the kid's father so they were mortal enemies. It was altogether different. The pull of the land remained the same, however. Cinnebar. He cleared his mind when a dog barked up ahead where the squares of pale light were. At first the dog barked in a questioning, curious way. Moments later, when Jason reined up and sat motionless studying the buildings the dog barked more savagely. Jason paid no more attention to him than the Cinnebar men did; ranch dogs bark at coyotes, at 'possums and skunks and 'coon and badgers most of the summer nights. Sometimes at a wolf or a deer. The animal's tongueing went shrill with excitement then dropped to a lower, more persistent bay.

There was a light in the kitchen or dining hall of the main house and one in the bunkhouse. That was as it should be. Jason rode in closer and the dog's racket turned to a half-snarl as he caught sight of the strange rider. Someone bellowed out the bunkhouse window for him to "Shut up, dammit!" and he subsided a little.

Jason dismounted, stood beside his horse thinking. Jenks was there, he was sure of that. He wanted him without dragging his entire crew into the scuffle if he could get him that way, however, so he led the animal

157

far out around the main house until he was back in the area where he'd tied his horse before, then he started forward towards the back of the house, also as he'd done before. The big gun rode in his fist, thumb hooked crookedly over the hammer.

There were two voices in the kitchen. They rose and fell with the sounds of argument. Jason made no attempt to listen, only to make out the area they came from. The back half of the kitchen, which was good. When he stepped up onto the planking near the door a big tendon in the back of his hand bulged. The gun-hammer raised, its thin firing pin poised lethally. Jason drew back the door and entered the room. Lamplight as bright as any he'd seen nearly blinded him. He saw the two men turn, stiffen, eyes widen and jaws swing slack.

"Good luck the first time," he said softly, dark eyes swimming in brightness. "I didn't think I'd find you right away, Jenks."

Burton didn't speak. Neither he nor the cook, Obie, moved. Jason's face was as blank as stone, his mouth as unrelenting. "Obie; use your right hand. Take his gun out and drop it."

Obie moved to obey, but reluctantly, and Jenks growled something inaudible at him. Obie's hand hung in the air. Jenks swore a little then said, "What the hell d'you think you're doing?"

"I'm going to walk you out of here, for one thing," Jason said. "After that it all depends on you. Go on, Obie, take his gun."

158

"Hands off," Jenks said to the cook and Obie's arm stopped again. Burton's hard stare was unmistakable. The sudden running of dark blood under his skin heightened the murder in his eyes. "You aren't taking anyone anywhere, Jase. Remember what I told you the last time you came out here looking for trouble; all I got to do is holler. Just one yell and you're a goner."

"Like Harry is?"

"Yeah," Burton said, "like Harry is."

"Go ahead and holler," Jason said. "There's a posse around Cinnebar, go ahead and holler. A man horses me once, Jenks, it's his fault. If he does it the second time and gets away with it, it's my fault. I came prepared this time."

"Where's your authority?"

Jason wagged his gun. "Here in my hand. If that isn't good enough Houston Mabry's out there with the posse. You're going back in for shooting Harry Mather."

"I didn't shoot anyone, you damned fool."

"It's all the same; if you didn't someone on Cinnebar did. Obie — take that gun off him."

"Steady," Burton said and for the third time the cook's hand hung undecided midway between him and his employer.

Jason's black eyes flamed. "*Shed that gun!*"

But Burton moved away from the cook, sidled away slowly, well out of the cook's reach, then he suddenly stopped and a crafty look spread over his face and he shrugged. "All right; you got the drop. Come take it, Obie."

Jason was puzzled by the abrupt change of heart. He shifted his gaze from Burton only when Obie took the gun out of its holster and let it fall. The last echo hadn't died away when Burton turned abruptly and walked towards the parlour door. "Go ahead," he said over his shoulder. "Shoot an unarmed man."

Jason swore and lunged after him. Obie back-pedalled and fell over a chair. Burton broke into a sprinting run through the darkened part of the house and Jason saw him for a fleeting second when he wrenched open the door and burst into the yard yelling at the top of his voice.

When Jason was out in the yard he saw a long shadow go around the corner of the house. Another long yell went up. From within the bunkhouse men answered Burton's shout and fury obscured Jason's vision. Men hollered questioningly and fanned out from the bunkhouse and in the darkness behind Jason a rifle boomed. He threw himself sideways, tripped over some stones that bordered a long untended flowerbed and fell flat. He lay there listening. Burton was making for the bunkhouse from the sounds of his voice and as Jason's rage cooled his disgust grew. He should have cracked Jenks over the head when he first saw him; it was all past now. The very thing all of them had wanted to avoid, he'd done; aroused Cinnebar.

The night grew ominously silent and Jason edged deeper into the flowerbed afraid to move now. There would be at least five sets of eyes probing for him. A stubby figure made a dash for the barn and Jason let him go. If he fired it would draw at least a half dozen shots in his direction. He rolled up on his side, got both legs under him and pushed his gun out, waiting for the rider he surmised would explode from the barn. When he came, bent low and pouring in the hooks, Jason drew a long bead, held his breath a second and squeezed off the shot. At the same time he leapt up and fled around the west corner of the house, flattened back into the siding and darkness.

The horse piled up in a flurry of man and horse. The animal never moved after he fell. The rider lay still for a long time, too, then he pushed himself upright, hung there a second and slowly fell back to earth.

Gunshots came from many directions. They struck the house above the flowerbed he'd been in with a vicious finality. Jason studied each flash of gunfire, decided the only thing to do was retreat. He felt his way along the house, backing, backing, until his fingers found the corner of the wall and he dropped low, peered around into the gloom and saw something white whisk up onto the back porch and guessed that Obie was there and regardless of what Obie had told him about not even owning a gun, there had been one rifleshot from behind when he was chasing Burton that could only have come from the cook.

There was a clearing directly behind the house for perhaps four hundred feet. Grass, curled and trampled low. No brush, trees, not even an out-house. If Obie was just a fair shot he couldn't miss a target as large as Jason, running across there. Around in front Burton's voice, ringing with savagery and triumph called out: "Close in!"

Jason went flat and crawled due west. It was open country but the house cast a dingy shadow and if he could get out far enough he'd have acres of country to manoeuvre in. Then he remembered the moon; it would be up shortly. They'd potshoot him like a tethered turkey when they could cutline him against the dun-brown grass and earth.

But he crawled anyway. There was no other way. Crawled with sweat stinging his eyes and helpless anger churning behind his belt.

He heard a rider thunder out of the yard, rolled over to see and caught a glimpse of the man, bent low and urging, on the animal's back, then the barn cut him off. Houston would have to take care of that one. He crawled farther and finally squirmed around to face the yard and house and pressed low in the trampled grass feeling huge and naked.

Far out two carbines exploded almost simultaneously and back by the house a voice called out in a high key. When the answer came Jason recognized the voice. He placed Jenks by the sound but didn't dare risk an exploratory shot.

Then riders were coming. He could hear them in the ground, feel the reverberations under him. It would be Houston; by God it had better be. If Jenks had gotten word out — but he couldn't have, not so soon. A long halloo boomed through the night, then another farther south, more calls, some repeated, until the night was full of them. Over the crescendo of yells a Cinnebar rider ripped out a scalding curse and cried out for Burton.

162

"There's a posse out there. Posse or an army, Jenks."
"Never mind them" the answer went back. "Five hundred dead for Anderson. Get him."

Jason had his chin on the ground. There were no gunshots only the steadily increasing thunder of oncoming riders, then the riders began to halloo again and that time back in the yard two guns flamed out, turned eastward away from Jason. Little sharp stabs of flame blew into the darkness and Jason's fear subsided until a slow-growing paleness filled the world as the blind moon came indifferently, slowly, majestically, up over the land. Then Jason was desperate. His momentary respite might be broken any instant. Cinnebar might be facing the posse but there was at least one among them who wouldn't forget the big man beyond the house. He watched the ground lighten with almost hypnotised fascination and when the bedlam up by the house broiled into a fury of sound he got up and ran anglingly southeast, trying to get back where his horse was without going any closer to the yard. He was panting from the exertion when he heard a rider racing parallel to him and twisted his head as he ran, feeling it must be a posseman.

When the horse swung into sight, rider erect, gun riding high in his fist, Jason's heart was crashing against his ribs and breath pumped in and out of him like a bellows.

The little clump of brush and trees wasn't far ahead. He could see it, was widening his stride when he heard the horse change leads and threw another look backwards. The rider had seen him, was coming

163

straight for him and his head was thrust forward, the gun tracking Jason. In a burst of recognition Jason threw himself sideways and earthward. The rider fired and the bullet thudded close by. Jason snapped a wild shot and rolled as fast as he could, almost whirled into the brush, felt its tearing branches with vast relief. Another bullet struck close. Jason didn't bother to reply. He burrowed deeper until he was well hidden, then he sat perfectly still listening. The horseman swung by without slackening his stride and poured three fast shots into the brush. Jason went low gripping his gun. After the last shot he was motionless, waiting. The sound diminished down the land. Jason raised up, saw the far blur of movement and estimated the distance, holstered his gun and leapt to his feet, ran to his own animal, jerked the tie loose and flung himself aboard. His heart was thudding with tremendous force. Jenks Burton wanted to make it a personal score; fine.

Behind him the tumult subsided, overhead the lonely moon swam in a purple sea and far ahead Burton was audible but invisible. Around him the range was ghostly brown, hushed and ancient looking. Twice he startled little herds of wet cows who swung to face him, heads low, their calves trembling, poised for flight.

He halted once when the sound of Burton came from the west. Paused and listened, waited until he was positive then swung his horse westerly also. Riding slower now, no longer even hoping he might overtake Cinnebar's owner, he wanted to keep the sound of his horse placed and track him that way. Gradually Burton's course angled northerly making a big half-circle around Cinnebar and lining out due north. Jason loped steadily after him and when his horse began to tilt and labour he knew which slope they were riding over. Beyond would be Willow Creek and west from there would be Will Saunders' place.

He halted on the lee of the hill, dismounted and let his horse blow. Burton might be going to Will for help. He might be going there to hole-up too. No; Jenks wasn't the holing-up kind. He might take Saunders and slope or he might just want Saunders to aid him in rousing the ranchmen. He looked at his horse. The animal was fairly well recovered; a thumb under the cinch, reins, mane, and a spring and he was astride. Whatever Jenks would do afterward, first he would rouse Will.

Threading his way through the willows Jason wished he'd brought a carbine with him. Saunders would surely have at least one. A pistol was useless against a Winchester. When he'd gone as far as he dared a long open space separated him from the distantly squared blocks against the tan earth that were Saunders' buildings. He strained to hear, no sound rewarded him. He twisted, looking towards the near side of the slope, no possemen. When he'd righted again in the saddle there was a wavering light up at the Saunders' place. If Burton and Saunders forted up, if they rode to rouse their friends, or if they fled, it was up to him to deter or stop them. Whatever must be done he had to do it alone. The thought irritated him. What would take the Holbrook men so long back at Cinnebar?

The light bobbed steadily as though someone were carrying it. Jason grunted a dour curse. If they were outside it would mean they were getting horses. An anxious survey of the country up by the ranch buildings showed no cover at all. He dismounted, smothered a quick-rising feeling of helplessness at being afoot again, left his horse hidden in the willows and started forward. They wouldn't see him until he was close which was a small consolation.

The moonwash was like pale silver. Silence as deep and engulfing as the night itself lay everywhere and only the steady crunching of his boots over the brittle grass, the faint tinkle of his spurs, marked Jason's advance. When he was close enough to feel a warning, well within carbine range, he stooped low and froze as the lantern came bobbing from behind the house. Two vague silhouettes showed now and then when the light splashed over them. He heard a horse blow its nose, a drowsy bird chirp with shrill querulousness then the faint rattle of several short words came down the night, indistinguishable. He crept closer, palmed his gun and knelt.

The moonlight helped him discern a horse standing beside a pile of saddlery near the front of the house. That would be a re-mount for Jenks Burton. Both men were inside where the light shone. He took time to punch out the expended casing from his gun and plug in a replacement, look around again and wonder what the hell was keeping Mabry and the others.

The rattle of reins chains caught his attention. One of the men was working beside the horse. Moonlight reflected dully off a worn seating-leather as a saddle was thrown across the animal's back. Jason dropped down on his belly, inched closer and kept his gun extended. He breathed shallowly and a sense of urgency nagged at him. When he knew he was within range he looked for a place to hide after he shot. There was nothing closer than the creek half a mile southward. He licked his lips. Had to keep them there as long as he could. Had to. But if they weren't half blind they'd make him out easily, black against the earthy tan, as soon as he fired. He had a quick, wincing vision of AnnaLee's face and closed it out of his mind. There was no other way.

He pushed the gun up, steadied it and drew a long bead on the man standing at the horse's head, curled his finger, tightened it and the night exploded with a lancing tongue of flame, a thunderous explosion and a booming yell of astonishment. Then Jason rolled. Went sideways rolling as fast as he could with his mind cleared of everything but expectation. The answering shot was a long time coming. It struck a rock nearby and careened overhead with a frightening scream. He stopped rolling and darted a wild look up towards the buildings. The horse was trotting away saddled but un-bridled, head high, tail out, snorting. The lantern was out and there wasn't any sign of men or movement. He began to roll again. Two shots threw dirt on him. He swore because two shots coming at the same time meant he hadn't hit the man he'd aimed at. When two more shots jarred the night they straddled him and he stopped rolling long enough to thumb off another shot, aiming at a window where flame had been. Instantly the other gun went off. A great spume of dust flew up on his left. He rolled again.

When he felt the earth spilling away under him a little he paused again. There was no grass where he lay and the smell of horses was strong. Dust inches thick rose in his nostrils. He was in a wallowed-out bowl that horses had used to roll in for a long time. It was several inches lower than the surrounding ground. Anything was better than nothing. He stopped rolling, choked on the dust, spat and came to rest on his stomach. The house was clearly visible. He raised his gun and fired at the partly open door. The sound of it slamming against the inner wall came sharply into the ensuing silence. From a corner of the house a carbine spat at him. One of them was outside. That meant somebody was trying for another horse; going to make a run for it. The sensation of urgency returned.

He reloaded his gun with grimy fingers and waited. When nothing happened he raised his head a little. No sounds, no movement. He threw a shot into the window, got no answer and thought both men had figured out that they were faced by only one man, not the entire posse. They weren't fighting, they were trying to escape.

Jason squirmed, black eyes slashing the night for a way to get around the house where the men would be. He had to; if they got horses, got mounted, had the whole night before them . . .

He rose out of the wallow and started towards the house in a clumsy, zig-zag run. No gunfire came. His confidence grew. He might be able to get . . . The explosion came like a sharp-edged stab of lightning and not from behind the house but off to his right and a little behind him. He spilled in a heap with a terrible pain spiralling upwards from below his belt somewhere. He rolled when he hit but his eyes were closed, teeth clenched. Wave after wave swept over him. Sickness filled his stomach and pain clamped a paralysing hold on his mind.

There were other shots and finally when they stopped a voice yelled from behind the house: "You get him?"

"I got him, goddamn him. I got him!"

CHAPTER
EIGHT

The triumph in that voice made Jason lift his head. A pounding fury mixed with anguish threshed behind his eyes. He thought surely the wound was fatal. Unless it was it couldn't hurt so much.

He got his gun forward and laid it across an arm, waiting but the gunman didn't stand up where Jason could skyline him. Moments went by dragging their feet. The pain died down to a centralised sickening agony. He used his left hand to explore as much of his body as he could. The wound was in his right leg somewhere. That was a relief; he'd thought he must have been disembowelled from the feeling he'd had when he fell. He moved the leg a little and the agony began again. He let the leg remain still waiting for the sick feeling to pass. When it was gone his mind overcame its terror and with the knowledge that the injury wasn't fatal went about half of the pain.

He lay there for what seemed hours but couldn't have been over five minutes then he heard horses coming and a grim, humourless smile worked around the edges of his mouth. The posse.

But it wasn't. It was two horses coming from the direction of Saunders' house. Then he knew they had foxed him. The man who had shot him never intended to come up close to make sure he'd killed Jason. He had crept out to shoot him if he could and lie low until the other renegade came out with horses. Good strategy, Jason thought. One to keep me busy while the other one got things set for their escape. Real good. Just one thing wrong with it; I'm not dead.

The rider was moving eastward. Jason finally saw him, a soft blur of movement. He lifted his gun and the horseman turned suddenly and booted his horse into a lope going northward, beginning to make a big circle around the disputed territory. Jason grew desperate watching the ridden horse and led horse go beyond pistol range.

"Where are you — out there?"

"Down here," the answer came.

Jason's head followed the last voice. He heard the rider going towards it. There was no way he could get down there. He moved the throbbing leg and the pain increased only a little but the ache kept pace with his pulse and drained away his will to move. He fisted both hands and began to pull himself forward. Defeat came to him in that endeavour too. He heard the men call to one another again, then one swore with relief.

"Here; that's good. You got everything? Then let's ride."

Jason's spirit shrivelled, his resolve crumbled. He hadn't done anything he'd wanted to do. First at Cinnebar, now here. He let his head down on a filthy shirt-sleeve and didn't move for half an hour, or until he heard horsemen coming in a slogging trot. Heard

171

them dip down by the creek, curse their way through the stinging willows and emerge onto the range and spread out a little as they approached him. Then he tilted his gunbarrel and tugged off a shot, let the gun drop and raised his head, propped it on one arm.

Houston Mabry saw him first and leapt down. The others crowded around, an intent, peeringly silent little clutch of men. Jason said, "They got away almost half an hour ago. Two of them, riding east."

"Who; Jenks and Will?"

"I never got close enough to identify either of them. I don't know."

Mabry straightened up and brushed fingers across Eric Fundemeyer's sleeve. "You stay with Jase, Eric. Me'n the others'll go after them. All right?"

"Sure," Eric said. He dropped to one knee. "Where are you hurt, Jase?"

"In the goddamned leg," Jason said disgustedly. He clamped his teeth down when the merchant began probing. Eric turned away from the leg and looked at Jason's face. It was profiled. Jason watched the possemen mount up and lope away across the silvery night.

"That's a funny one, Jase," Eric said.

The black eyes lingered on the disappearing riders when Jason answered. "Yes; funny as a kick in the guts by an Army mule."

Eric got up and brushed off his knee. "Well; what I meant was the bullet didn't hit you at all."

That brought the dark, bitter face around. "Didn't? Something sure as hell did. It hurts like a — ."

172

"Sure it does. Your ankle's broken, Jase, but the bullet hit your bootheel and twisted your leg. The heel's plumb shot away. The twisting is what broke the ankle."

"Might as well hit me then," Jason said. "Eric; my horse's tied down there by the ford in the creek, back in the willows. If you'll get him we'll ride."

Eric hesitated a moment gazing at Jason, then he said, "Sure; be right back," and started for his mount.

Jason squirmed around until he was sitting up. He gazed at his lower leg like he hated it, then began to poke expended casings out of his gun and re-load it. By the time he'd finished Eric was back leading his horse. The pain began as soon as Eric's big arms hoisted Jason off the ground. Dust and dirt fell away from him and when Eric handed him his hat he crushed it down on his head indifferently.

Mounting was exquisite agony but he endured it and once astride found that by having Eric shorten his stirrup two holes the pain lessened when he kept the injured ankle with just a little pressure on it. He reined around and struck out easterly and Eric, dumbfounded, sat a moment watching him.

"Jason — where are you going?"

"Follow the posse."

Eric urged his horse forward, caught up and peered into the younger man's face. "Listen, Jason — let Houston do it. He'll catch them if they can be — ."

"I rode over a thousand miles to get where I am tonight, Eric, and I've made it plain to the world I'll be in at the kill. A busted ankle isn't going to stop me now."

"But — ."

"But hell!"

They rode steadily and in silence and the pain never left. Jason's forehead was beaded with sweat, his mouth was pulled down and flat, the lips bloodless. The smouldering blackness of his eyes matched the darkest shadows they rode through and he cursed silently because he knew he wouldn't be able to stand the pain of loping his horse.

They came to a creek where fluted walls of trees went regularly up the slope beyond. The horses drank and Eric got some water in Jason's hat and gave it to him. It tasted excellent. A pleasant aftermath was the coolness around his head as they rode on. When they were near the crest of the forested hilltop Jason turned to Eric.

"What happened back at Cinnebar?"

"Well; one of them got shot," Eric said, "another one had a horse shot from under him near the barn and he's pretty bad off. Broken collarbone I think. About a half mile out two of the boys caught another one riding for it and downed him. I mean — they shot the horse and captured the man. The others couldn't find Jenks and threw their guns down. Houston had them tied to horses, disarmed and sent back to Holbrook with a guard."

"It took long enough," Jason said through locked teeth. "I'd about given you fellers up."

Eric looked sideways at Jason and didn't speak.

They topped out and reined up. Down below in the faint light was an endless sea of dead grass. Jason sought movement and found none. His heart was like lead. He swore. "No telling where they are."

Eric slouched in the saddle, tried to make his voice soothing. "Houston'll stay after them. He'll bring them in, Jase."

The quiet tone irritated Jason. He turned, skirted along the crest, found a game trail and put his horse down it recklessly. The animal had to hunch down behind. Miniature cascading avalanches skittered downward and Eric, hesitating atop the rim, frowned in dislike then eased his own mount down the narrow trail.

Just before they hit the swells of land below the crest Jason threw a long, final glance out over the distance and the exact moment he was looking four red fireflies erupted dead ahead. He pulled up so sharply the horse threw his head and snorted. Listening, waiting, the faintest of echoes came; one, two, three, and four. He twisted in the saddle.

"Eric; they've got 'em straight ahead of us about three miles."

Eric answered through stiff lips and never lifted his eyes from the treacherous trail. "Good. Keep going," he said.

When they were riding stirrup over the undulating lower reaches an urge to hurry almost overwhelmed Jason. It seemed that his tired horse was creeping. He swung his head from side to side with restlessness. Was still doing it, like a hunting wolf, when he caught the distant drumming of hoofs and jerked erect trying to place the direction.

They were coming from the southeast in a diagonal way. Jason spoke without moving his head, concentrating and wondering whether it was a posseman or someone else. He threw up an arm, pointing.

"From over there, Eric. Hear it?"

"Yes, I hear it."

Jason dropped his glance, scanned the country closer and reined towards a clump of jack-pines with Eric trailing him. In among the trees his anxiety reached enough of an apex to make him temporarily forget the grinding throb in his ankle.

The rider was coming fast but just before he dipped into a gloomy arroyo and lifted out on the far side he slowed to a kidney-jolting trot and when he emerged from the arroyo Jason saw him.

The man was riding tired, shoulders slumped, head erect and wary but hanging a little. His horse shone under the pale light with a dull gloss of sweat. Eric said something in a sotto voice that Jason neither heard nor heeded. He felt for his gun and it wasn't there; the holster was gaping empty. Eric spoke again. Jason looked down in utter astonishment.

". . . Down that trail, Jason, that's what I've been telling you. I got it before — ."

There was no time to reach over for the gun Eric was holding out. Jason's fingers hurried with the frantic speed of a hairless spider and the ties fell away from his lariat. A loop dropped out, hung low beside him, fingers hefted the hang of it, found the balance right.

"Eric; cover him. If he goes for his gun shoot him."

"Yes," Eric said in a dutiful but strangled way. "Can you see who it is?"

"Will Saunders. Now watch him an' don't shoot the wrong man."

There was no time after that because Saunders was kicking his horse out into a lope again. Jase was poised. When the second was right he jumped his horse out of the little trees and the lariat sang in a lazy circle gathering momentum. Saunders' grey face turned for a fleeting second. The moon spanked across it showing the utter astonishment, the widened little eyes, the glazed expression, the slack lips, then the loop was lifting and falling with infinite grace and Saunders' breath exploded as he ducked low to escape the noose and went for his gun. His horse shied at the sudden apparition bearing down on them and Saunders, already bending, already off-balance, lost a stirrup. His right leg shot out and forward from the sideways leap of the horse and Jason saw the wide loop falter, descend, and miss its mark, go lower, catch at the saddle and slide away, go still lower, then he felt it snug down on something and a tremor passed down the length of it all the way to Jason's saddlehorn where it was secured by a hard-and-fast-knot.

A mushrooming burst of blue-crimson flame stunned Jason, blinded him. He felt his panicked horse tilt, his head bog, and the beast's backbone exploded under the saddle throwing Jason end over end.

From behind him another gun went off, twice. A man screamed and through his red-froth of pain Jason's mind winced from the terror in that scream. The earth was cool on his cheek. He fought to hold consciousness, pushed at the ground to sit up and hung there, head down, arms stubbornly stiffened, until the wild seconds were past and Eric was beside him, big, powerful hands at his armpits for the second time that night, lifting.

"Can you stand, Jase? 'Hear me; can you stand?"

"Got to lean."

"All right. Here now; lean on my horse. That's it. Don't let go of him or we'll both be afoot. I've got to find your animal."

"Better take yours," Jason said thickly. "Can't catch him afoot."

"Yes I can." Eric's voice had a strange quality to it. Jason fought his head up, opened his eyes and looked into the merchant's face. Eric put a heavy hand on his shoulder. "Just hold on, Jase, I'll be right back. Just a few minutes."

"Want to lie down, Eric."

The merchant shook his head at him. "Don't do it, you'll pass out."

"Did he hit me? Wasn't twenty feet away when he fired."

"No; I think he nicked your horse though. He bucked you off, Jase. Now hang on there, boy; keep your wits."

Jase focused his eyes on Eric's wide back, watched the older man start walking in a stilted way northeastward and a thousand yards or so beyond there was movement. He was instantly aware of danger. From some mysterious source within him came a quick

178

gush of energy. He dropped his hand automatically to the empty holster and opened his mouth to call, to warn Eric.

"Eric! Something's over there!"

The big man turned sideways. His voice came back in the same forced, stilted way. "I know. It's your horse."

"Horse," Jason said to himself. "Where's Saunders?" Anxiety for Eric persisted until he heard the merchant talking. The words were barely heard but Jason could make out enough to know. Eric was talking to his horse. Then the merchant bent, still talking, soothing the animal. Jason guessed he was untangling him. The lariat, of course, it had snagged on brush or a rock or some jackpines. He sighed. Good thing; if the lariat hadn't snagged he'd have been in a bad way. He watched Eric as the trepidation dissolved.

The merchant had Jason's horse by the reins, was leading him out of the snarl of brush he was in. Then Eric stopped, standing very erect, very motionless. After a moment he turned, worried the hard-and-fast-knot off the saddlehorn and tossed it aside. Jason was puzzled by that. He'd never seen a lariat so tangled that it couldn't be untangled. Why throw aside a perfectly good rope?

Then Eric was coming towards him again, close beside the horse. When he came up the moonlight showed his face. It was ashen, the eyes wide and still looking. He offered Jason the reins and turned, ran a hand up Jason's horse's neck, touched a dark-shiny spot and in an unnatural way said: "That's where the bullet nicked him. I don't see how it missed you."

Intuitively Jason knew. He glanced at the horse's neck and looked steadily at Eric and he knew what was out there. "Will?" he said.

"Yes. When your horse bucked you off and bolted the lariat was around Will's right ankle. He got jerked off and dragged."

"He's over there?"

"Yes." Eric took the gun out of his waistband and held it out. "Here. What I was trying to tell you was that I saw it on that steep trail we came down, scooped it up as I went by. It must have fallen out."

Jason took the gun, holstered it and pulled his horse in close, balanced himself on his left leg and gritted his teeth, swung up and over, eased down into the saddle and looked down for the stirrup, found it and very gently put his right foot in, exerted the smallest amount of pressure and felt the pain lessen. He heard Eric mount behind him as he turned, walked his horse back over the route Eric had led him. Reined up and looked down on Will Saunders' dead, frozen looking face with the moonlight shining in brittle paleness off the open eyes.

Eric stopped just behind him. He wasn't looking down at all. Jason finally turned his horse. "He must have hit that tree there, or the half-buried rock next to his head."

"It was the rock," Eric said.

180

They rode slowly down the land and Jason didn't speak again until they had put five miles behind them. "Eric; do you believe in the Law of Retribution?"

Eric said, "I don't know, Jason."

"In the back of my mind," Jason said slowly, "was an idea. I wanted to catch Saunders out and lynch him. Hang him with my rope for murdering the judge."

Eric looked over at him. "I guess I understand," he said, and that was all until they came upon Houston Mabry and three riders jogging back towards them. The deputy marshal hauled up and peered at them a moment before he relaxed and began to fumble with his cigarette papers and tobacco sack.

"You see anyone come up this way, Jase? Eric?"

"If you mean Will Saunders," Eric said, "he's dead."

Houston's fingers stopped moving. "Dead?"

"Jason roped him. He shot at Jason and hit his horse . . ."

"Drug to death?" Houston asked softly, watching both their faces. Eric nodded and Houston licked the paper, crimped the end and stuck the thing in his mouth, flicked a match, inhaled, snapped the match and dropped it. "Hell of a way to die," he said, "even for Saunders."

Jason brushed it aside with words. "Where's Jenks? Did you get him?"

"Nope. We had 'em both boxed up and Will made a break for it, got clean away and came up this way. I was after him when a rider came up and told me the other one'd gotten away too. I went back but Jenks was gone for sure." The cigarette tip glowed then dulled. "The rest of the boys're still after him. I brought these fellers back with me to see if we could catch Will."

"We don't want anything to happen to Jenks, though," Jason said to Mabry. "If he goes out we'll never know the answers to a lot of things."

Houston nodded slowly, thoughtfully, then raised his eyebrows. "How do you feel, Jase?"

"Lousy. Like my leg's been cut off at the throat."

Houston flickered a small smile and nodded. "What you reckon we ought to do now?"

"Do?" Jason said, surprised. "Why keep after him until we get him."

Mabry studied the larger man's face and sighed. "It's a good thing folks can't see their own faces," he said. "All right; let's go back where we left Jenks and see if we can pick up any sign of him, which I doubt like hell. If it was closer to dawn . . ."

They rode slowly and the ghost of Will Saunders rode with them. Each mind was secretly closeted with it. What a hell of a way to die.

Houston said, "We broke him, Jase. Busted him wide open. There isn't an idiot dumb enough in the country to throw in with him now. He's a lone wolf and when we get back I'll have his goddamned description on a flock of posters from here to Cheyenne. Buck Holbrook law, will he. Incite lynchings and have lawmen shot, will he!"

Jason didn't answer. He was hoarding his strength because he knew better than any of them he wasn't going to be able to hold out much longer.

When they got back where the fight had taken place Jason got Eric to help him dismount. He lay full length under the stars and relaxed slowly, as the pain dulled. Closed his eyes and lay inertly while the others sought for sign, which he knew perfectly well they wouldn't be able to find at night. Even on a full-moon night. When someone knelt beside him he opened his eyes, rolled his head a little. It was Eric.

"Want me to make you a cigarette, Jase?"

"No thanks." With an attempt at humour he said: "Now'd be a good time for me to quit smoking, wouldn't it?"

"Yeah. They haven't found anything."

"Did you expect them to?"

Eric shrugged. "I'm not a manhunter I'm a storekeeper."

"If Indians can't do it at night what chance do we stand?"

"None, I suppose. What'll we do now?"

Jason's gaze strayed past Eric's face, far out and beyond where the soft sky was. "Only two things we can do, Eric. Camp right here and trail him come dawn, or go back to town, get fresh horses and come back."

Eric shook his head. "Not you, Jason. We've been talking about it. I'm going to take you back where Tobey Harding can fix your leg and two of the others are going back with us and trail some other horses back. Houston and the rest will wait here."

Jason regarded the far-away sky dully and nodded his head. *Got one of them; the main one I guess, so what difference does it make if I'm not in on it when they get the other one — the brains.* "All right, Eric," he said. "Any time."

When Eric led his horse back from a spring nearby freshly watered Jason had managed to hobble over where a spindly little oak grew and hold himself erect. They mounted in silence and started southward. Two of the Holbrook possemen trotted up behind them, slowed to a walk and followed.

Jason felt a little better and only once did he have to lock his jaws. An overlooked arm of a scraggly chaparral bush lashed backwards off his horse's shoulder and struck his ankle. The pain returned with a vengeance and brought nausea with it. His back ached too, where he'd landed after being bucked off his horse but it was a comparatively minor thing.

The town lights swung into place in the distance, not many for it was late, but enough to show warmth. Eric heaved a great, rattling sigh. "She'll either be so tickled to see me she'll cry or she'll be so relieved she'll be fighting mad."

One of the possemen chuckled. It was a pleasant, warm sound.

Eric swung his big head and grinned quizzically at Jason. "But we're back and alive and that's something, isn't it?"

The black eyes were sober and wracked appearing. "Yes, I guess so. Every hour we sit around he's getting farther away; too."

Eric's smile flickered and died. He turned back moodily and contemplated the town. Quietly he said, "And they talk about Dutchmen being pig-headed."

184

The doleful way he said it, gravely serious, brought two crashing roars of spontaneous laughter from the possemen. Even Jason's haggard face showed a glint of appreciation. Only Eric remained solemn. He'd meant it to be serious, expressing exactly the thought behind it.

"Well, Jason — you took care of one of them. The right one at that." He paused in thought. "And they'll get the other one. I'd bet my life on it."

"Maybe," Jason said. "Eric; have you had days — or nights — when everything just seemed to go wrong?"

"Yes, everyone has days like that."

"This night was mine. First at Cinnebar then at Saunders' place, then getting a busted ankle, then that business with the rope and Will — finally when Jenks got away. Nothing turned out like I wanted it to."

"You wanted Will and you got him," Eric said quietly.

"Not — well — it doesn't make any difference." The black eyes grew saturnine. "Now I'll have to get Doc out of bed, to boot."

"He doesn't mind that, it's his business. Besides, I think that after all these years he's used to it."

Jason made a dry laugh. "The way I feel right now Eric, I could sleep for a year and if anyone woke me up I'd shoot them."

"No," Eric said in that same gravely stolid way. "Not AnnaLee you wouldn't shoot."

Jason's thoughts stopped writhing, froze still in his mind and hung suspended over her name, then slowly descended and closed around it. "I guess you're right," he said as they let their horses pick their own way through the upper and outlying reaches of the town.

Tobey Harding wasn't in bed at all. He was smoking his pipe and reading by the bell-topped parlour lamp when Eric got heavily down and stumped across the hard-walk, through the gate and up onto the porch. The doctor opened the door before Eric's raised fist touched it. He blinked up at Fundemeyer owlishly. "Well; at least you're alive," he said sharply. "That's something."

"Jason's out there, Tobey. I think his ankle's broken."

Harding peered past the big merchant and ducked his head up and down in a grim way. "Is that all? Well; bring him in, Eric. Oh, Eric; any others?"

"Not that I know of."

Harding blinked again. "You'd know, wouldn't you? You were with them, weren't you?"

Fundemeyer waved his big hand. "Later, Tobey," he said wearily and started back down the porch steps.

The two possemen helped Jason off his horse. Would have helped him into the house but he waved them away. Tobey Harding came down to slide under Jason's other arm. He and Eric got the injured man into the house and seated in the parlour chair near the lamp. The doctor straightened up, took his pipe out of the ashtray and stuck it unlighted into his mouth.

"Fine," he said to Jason. "I like this kind of a broken ankle. Do you know why? Because I can cut your boot off and the forlorn looks riders get when I ruin their boots always repays me a little for the inconvenience of mending their bodies. You see?"

186

Jason didn't answer and Eric sank down heavily on a leather sofa, rubbed his eyes and yawned prodigiously.

The doctor worked in silence, quick, strong fingers moving with the grace that goes only with confidence. When he had the boot and sock off and was studying the livid purple flesh he said, "Tell me about it, Jason."

"Not much to tell."

Harding's sardonic eyes shot upwards. "Tell me anyway. Talk about it. Say anything you want to but talk about it. It will serve two purposes, y'see. One; get the fog out of your mind, clean out the festering thoughts. The other thing — this is going to hurt like Christ Almighty and I want as much of your mind off it as I can get. Now talk."

Jason talked and gasped and went limp in the chair twice before Tobey Harding had the rough splints on the ankle, the swathes of bandaging bound around and around with professional skill and the pain killed with a mild injection of morphine. By then he knew all he would ever know about the fight at Cinnebar, the brief scuffle at Willow Creek, the death of Will Saunders and all the rest of it. He turned away from Jason only when a repetitive and stentorian rumble, rich and bubbling, began its rhythmic and ragged regularity in the vicinity of his sofa. Eric was dead to the world, head on one arm, booted feet dangling over the other arm of the sofa, sleeping the sleep of utter and total exhaustion.

Doctor Harding stood up, knocked dottle out of his pipe, re-filled it and sucked in a big lungful of smoke, exhaled it and nodded critically at Jason. "Something I've always marvelled at, Jason. The stamina of your family. Your mother's strength of spirit was phenomenal. Your father's too. Now your's." He lifted his shoulders and let them fall. "Remarkable. I don't suppose I'll ever understand why some people have it and some don't, but I've certainly learned to recognize it when I see it."

Jason sat perfectly motionless for quite a while after the pain was gone, then, reluctantly, he gripped the arms of the chair and heaved himself upright. "Better get home, Doc," he mumbled. "Be around to see you in the morning."

But Doctor Harding was shaking his head. "You can't do it, Jase, not in the shape you're in."

"What do you mean?"

"Just that. Wait until I get my hat."

Jason watched Harding scuttle from the room and return in an instant with a nondescript headpiece athwart his grizzled locks. He let Harding take his arm and only hesitated once, at the doorway, when Eric's cyclonic snoring rose to a rip-saw crescendo, then slid down into a palpitating moan.

"What about him. Doc? We'd better get him home."

"Yes, sure. We'll go by his house and tell Mrs. Fundemeyer where he left his hulk. Come on."

Jason tested the ankle, found that it would support a little of his weight and forgot that the morphine was still working as he hobbled along on Doctor Harding's arm. When they turned northward Jason's eyes automatically searched out the dark bulkiness of the Downey house. He was startled to see a light burning steadily in the parlour. In a musing way, he said, "She isn't still up, is she?"

Harding shot him a reproachful scowl. "Half the town's still up. Women don't go to bed and sleep when their men are out in a posse, Jase."

Harding stumped along supporting Jason, right past the Fundemeyer house, all the way to the corner of Lincoln Street where the hard-walk ended, turned in at the Downey gate and struggled around to support his massive patient and close the gate at the same time, and Jason forgot how god-awful he looked, filthy, bruised, covered with horse-wallow dust, ragged shirt and torn trousers. He remembered only that AnnaLee would be there. Was thinking that when a furtive, fluid shadow snagged his vision at the corner of the house and in a rush the old fear and tenseness was back. Blood pounded up from his heart and beat in his ears.

He saw the shadow scurry to the corner of the house then jerk erect, pause, glide around the corner and disappear for an instant. A brief second later a dark object appeared slowly around the base of the house close to the ground. Someone . . .

Jason's strength succoured him. With a violent blow he sent Tobey Harding sprawling at the same instant realization burst inside his head. Who would want to skulk around the Downey place? Who had a deadly reason to want to exact one last drop of vengeance from the people within the house? He was throwing himself sideways when the explosion came. The slug ripped high with an unearthly scream and Jason's gun bucked hard against his thumb-pad. Then silence for a moment, but only for a moment because Doctor

Harding let out a startled bleat and he began beating his coat pockets for a tiny belly-gun he carried.

Jason thumbed back the dog and waited. The head was gone, so was the gun. "Here, Doc," he said tightly. "You take this side of the house and I'll take the other." He swung his head. "You have a gun haven't you?"

Almost plaintively Harding said, "Well; I *did* have — somewhere — dammit all."

Jason got up and started for the corner of the house. There was a roaring sound in his head. No shot greeted him. At the edge of the building he flattened, listening. Somewhere over behind Lincoln Street a man called out and several dogs burst into a bedlam of excitement. He heard footsteps inside. A door slammed and Jason catapulted himself around the corner and crouched. The assassin wasn't there. He hobbled as fast as he could to the back corner and listened. Aside from the sounds of the neighbourhood coming awake there was nothing to encourage him at all. He lay flat and peered around the wall. No movement. As he was getting to his feet he heard a noise inside the house, a shrill cry that galvanised him into action. He made his way to the back porch, up it to the door and wrenched the knob, found the door wasn't altogether closed and burst into the kitchen just as a gunshot sounded.

Without waiting he hastened through the kitchen into the parlour, swung right through an ajar door with the strong carbolic smell in his nostrils and the snout of his hand-gun was low and swinging when he saw AnnaLee, stiff, staring, to one side of her brother's bed and Bob himself, the little under-and-over .41 almost hidden in his fist, staring at the crumpled form on the bedroom floor.

Jason eased his hammer off cock, holstered the gun and bent low in one movement. Jenks Burton was face down. A soggy lumpiness responded when Jason swung him over onto his back searching for the wound.

"Higher," Bob said, "up by his head somewhere — I think."

Jason saw it when Burton's head lolled. The ear was almost entirely gone. A deep groove scored the flesh. Jason let his breath out slowly, straightened up and groped for a chair, sank down onto it and looked at Bob Downey. "I'm glad you didn't *try* to do that," he said, "because if you had you've have killed him."

"Isn't he dead?"

Jason wagged his head slowly. "Fraction of an inch more and you'd have busted his head like a pumpkin. As it is you tore his ear off and creased him good." He looked up at AnnaLee. Her face was like new milk, pale and shiny. Her eyes went slowly to his own and a terrible shiver she couldn't control went through her. Jason smiled. "Let Doc in the front door will you?" Without answering she left the room and Jason gazed pensively at Burton again. Bob Downey was examining the little gun with awe, turning it over and over. Jason watched him a moment. "Funny thing, Bob," he said. "I took that gun from Burton's office at Cinnebar. He got shot by his own gun."

Doctor Harding came in with a ruffled, almost angry expression on his face. He ignored Jason and peered closely at Burton. "Well," he said caustically, "sewing up tag ends of ears doesn't cost much." He shot AnnaLee a glance. "The medicine he needs is the cheapest kind. Get me a pail of cold water, will you, AnnaLee?"

Jason watched when Harding trickled the water over Burton. Saw the cowman sputter back to consciousness and try to rise, fall back and stare at them all. He leaned on the chair.

"Jenks; who shot Bob Downey?"

"Shot," Jenks said and choked, coughed out water and tried to rise again. That time Doctor Harding held him down.

"Who shot him, Jenks?"

"Will. Will shot him."

"Who shot the marshal?"

"Ahhh . . . I did. Came out to make trouble. I — ."

"All right," Harding said sharply. "That's enough for now. AnnaLee — some black coffee all around?"

When she walked away Jason struggled up and followed her. Doctor Harding's sardonic eyes followed them, then he shook his head in a rueful and exasperated way, and grunted.

She turned to face him in the kitchen doorway and his name went past her lips like it was torn out of her. He braced himself, caught her close, felt the first spasm go through her, felt the softer ones when she cried in a terrible and awesome way, without making a sound.

"It's all over, AnnaLee — all over."

ISIS publish a wide range of books in large print, from fiction to biography. Any suggestions for books you would like to see in large print or audio are always welcome. Please send to the Editorial department at:

ISIS Publishing Ltd.
7 Centremead
Osney Mead
Oxford OX2 0ES
(01865) 250 333

A full list of titles is available free of charge from:
Ulverscroft large print books

(UK)
The Green
Bradgate Road, Anstey
Leicester LE7 7FU
Tel: (0116) 236 4325

(Australia)
P.O Box 953
Crows Nest
NSW 1585
Tel: (02) 9436 2622

(USA)
1881 Ridge Road
P.O Box 1230, West Seneca,
N.Y. 14224-1230
Tel: (716) 674 4270

(Canada)
P.O Box 80038
Burlington
Ontario L7L 6B1
Tel: (905) 637 8734

(New Zealand)
P.O Box 456
Feilding
Tel: (06) 323 6828

Details of **ISIS** complete and unabridged audio books are also available from these offices. Alternatively, contact your local library for details of their collection of **ISIS** large print and unabridged audio books.